My Pride, His Prejudice
Austen in Love, Book 1

by Jenni James

Cover design copyright © 2015 by Jenni James

SERENITY BROOKE PRESS

This book is dedicated to:

M.M. Bennets, my dear, dear friend. May the heavens shine brighter ever after.

Acknowledgements:

I would like to thank my sweet, handsome, playful hubby for all the wonderful Will Darcy material. You have added a sparkle to my life I never thought I'd feel. I love you.

Table of Contents

CHAPTER ONE:

"Excuse me? What did you say?" Eliza's heart rate tripled as she nervously flipped her long blond hair over her shoulder. It was way too late at night to be dealing with this. How in the world could this be happening? Nothing made sense. Nothing.

The handsome man knelt down on one knee in front of her on her entranceway tile and reached into his chest pocket. "I was saying—"

"No!" She put her fingers over his to prevent him from pulling out the inevitable ring. A warm, solid hand met hers, and Eliza quickly pulled away. "I . . . er . . . I just meant that maybe you shouldn't get too excited. I really don't think we'd work out as a couple."

Will Darcy, Salt Lake City's hottest and wealthiest bachelor, gave her a strange look. "What do you mean, we wouldn't work out?"

There was no way he was serious. She wanted to roll her eyes, but didn't. "I'm assuming you haven't had very many women turn you down for anything, have you?"

He cleared his throat and slowly made his way back to a standing position. "So … are *you* turning me down?"

Now that they were both standing, she couldn't help but notice just how very tall he was, or how broad his shoulders actually were. Good grief—no wonder so many women fell for his charm. The man was like a cover-model-movie-star-god. Ugh. She hated his type. Eliza took a deep breath. "Yes, I am. But I'd like to thank you for the … er . . . amazing honor this is."

"Wait." He tilted his head. "Are you saying you had no idea I felt this way?"

She nearly choked. "About me? That you wanted to marry me? Uh—no." Like that would've ever entered her mind. They could barely stand to be around each other, let alone snuggle next to each other at night. Oh. My. Word. She shuddered. That was the closest she would ever get to that image again. Yeesh.

He put his hands in his pockets and nodded. "Nice. I start to propose, and not only do you reject me, but you shudder as you do it."

Her jaw dropped slightly. What was going on? "What am I supposed to do? I thought you despised me. But more importantly than that—why? Why me? Why now?" Elizabeth looked around and raised her hands, palms up. There had to be a camera somewhere, right? "Is—is this a joke?"

"No, Eliza, it isn't a joke." He rubbed his face and stared off into the distance. She could see his emotional wall going up between them like an iron wedge.

He couldn't be serious. "Wait! Just answer me."

His dark brown eyes met hers. The black ring around his beautiful irises seemed softer tonight, almost like they were … She gasped. "You're crying?"

He winced. "Goodnight, Eliza." As he turned to leave, she grabbed the sleeve of his suit.

"Just a minute. Don't go yet." He refused to make eye contact again. "I have to understand why. This seems so surreal. If you're serious, please, explain to me. Weren't we—didn't we—haven't we always been enemies?" Her voice drifted off. She felt so lost and vulnerable all of a sudden. William Darcy was upset, and somehow her whole world began to slip like sand underneath her feet.

He glanced down. Her eyes followed his, down his well-fitted gray suit and purple tie, all the way to his sharp designer dress shoes and then to her entranceway tile beneath their feet. "I was never your enemy," he whispered.

She felt as though she'd been punched in the stomach. But she couldn't let this end here and now—she had to sort this out. "Yes, yes, you were. I overheard you telling Charles Bingley that I wasn't even good enough to date. How my presence annoyed you, since I wasn't someone trained by your father's company. How you didn't even want me in your office building, let alone as your consultant."

"Yes. I said that." He still looked down. His foot tapped slowly on the floor.

"And then you've gone about making my life awful these last ten months, trying anything you can to get me fired."

His head snapped up, and their eyes locked. This time, there was a blaze deep inside. "No. That's where you're wrong. I never wanted you gone. I'd hoped and prayed you'd be half the woman I realized you were. I knew you weren't afraid of me. I knew you'd tell me like it is. I knew you were the exact woman I needed to help this whole company progress. I didn't like it at first, but I knew it." He walked over and leaned his shoulder against the door. "However, eventually I went against my better judgment, everything I'd been trained in an office environment to do, and decided to form a relationship with my consultant—I saw you as a woman I had to date, had to get to know more, and eventually, the woman I had to love."

Her jaw dropped and she stepped back, though her eyes could not break their gaze. "Really? But . . .?"

"But what?" He shook his head. "Are you telling me you had no idea my feelings had changed? What about our lunches? Weren't those considered dates? And those business trips? I took you halfway around the world!"

Was she hearing him right? "Yeah, the lunches where we spent at least an hour and a half arguing over your ridiculous attempts to handle certain clients? And those business trips when I had to leave my plans behind and instead babysit you for days on end to make sure you didn't screw something up?"

"Babysit me?" He stepped forward. "Of all the—when you were the one who had no idea how to dress appropriately until you began working for me? You couldn't even attend a public function without somehow saying something crass or outrageous and nearly upsetting my guests. Yes, you, the wild card!" He pointed right at her. "That's right—I brought you along to babysit me." He folded his arms and attempted a laugh.

"Then why bring me?" She put her hands on her hips. "I knew you didn't like me. I knew you were too arrogant to see anything past your own nose—I knew it! I'm surprised you even managed to take the time to stand in my doorway now and ... and..."

"Propose?"

She straightened her back and lifted her chin. Was that what this really was? A proposal? Not some joke? "Yes, propose. You still haven't answered my question. Why me?"

"Yes, I did answer your question, though you're too afraid of being wrong to have heard what I really said." He ran his hands through his hair. "It doesn't matter. You've made it clear you think I'm some overbearing monster who doesn't deserve you anyway."

"Well, if you had ever showed me once that you cared about me, given me any sign at all how you really felt, maybe I wouldn't be in such shock right now."

He stepped toward her, all tall, dark, and handsome power. "Would it have made a difference?"

No. She wanted to have some chemistry with the man she married, not this conceited ego on a stick.

"No answer?"

She stalled. "Would *what* have made a difference?"

Will closed his eyes and sighed. "Never mind. It's obvious that we're going in circles now. Look, I'll see you in the office on Monday. That is, if you still plan on working for me."

Yeah, because this isn't awkward at all. "Of course."

"And let me apologize for my stupidity. We're clearly on two very different pages—something I'm relieved to see now. So thank you for your honesty."

Two different pages? Good grief, they weren't even in the same book! She smiled a tight smile. His arrogance was bugging her again. "Apology accepted."

"Good luck. I'm sure there's a guy out there you'll fall for eventually. Don't hold your breath, though. It might be awhile before you find one you actually like."

That was it. She snapped. "Goodnight." She pushed past him and opened the door. "The answer is no. Never."

As he left and she shut the door, she felt her whole body begin to tremble. Laying her head against the thick wooden surface, she realized that for no good reason at all, she felt like crying . . . and punching the door . . . but mostly like crying.

CHAPTER TWO:

Eliza closed her eyes and adjusted the phone tighter under her chin. "I know, Mom. I know. He's completely rich and single and hot. I know. Now, for like the hundredth time, I just don't feel like dating him." She flicked her blond hair to the side and slipped her feet into the adorable half boots she'd found on clearance the other day. Eliza clutched her purse while her mother continued to spew out the annoying perfections of Utah's most eligible bachelor.

"Yes, I avoid him. And I will continue to avoid him the longer I work there." Eliza rolled her eyes and tapped her foot as she listened to the older woman's disapproval.

Her mom would never stop. Eliza glanced at the small watch around her wrist. Ugh. She was late. After another quick look around her nearly pristine kitchen to make sure she had everything she needed, Eliza hastily put her half-empty mug of herbal tea in the sink, grabbed her keys, and headed out the door. After fiddling with the lock, she managed to make it to her car before her mom had actually convinced her that Will Darcy was worth the amount of energy it took to talk about him.

Funny thing is, her mom would never convince her.

And her mother would never forgive her if she knew that he had surprised her with a proposal the other day. There was absolutely no way she'd ever know, either.

"Okay, Mom, I've gotta go. Can't talk on the phone while I'm driving." It was a lame attempt, she knew it, but she honestly couldn't talk about her boss another second.

"Where's your Bluetooth?"

Eliza started up the car. "It broke. Okay. Really, gotta run. I love you, Mom. I'll call you later tonight. Bye." She set the phone down and pulled out of the driveway, then shook her head.

What was her mom's fascination with Will, anyway? Who cared if the guy had wealth—what about common decency? He had to be the most stuck-up man she'd ever met in her life, but for some reason, he found her irresistible. Or apparently, he *did* find her irresistible until she refused him.

It was now Monday morning, nine a.m. It had been two and a half days since Will had unexpectedly shown up on her front porch. She'd had the whole weekend to convince herself that she wasn't thinking about him—not really. At least, not the way anyone else would've been thinking about Will if they'd been in her shoes. But—ugh! Enough.

She pulled the car into her designated parking spot at the downtown Walker building. Eliza quickly made her way into the sleek lobby and up the elevator to the Revolutionary Innovations floor. The company owned buildings in nearly every major city in the U.S., and several overseas. However, there was something magical about the old Walker building, with its Edwardian architecture and lavish marble walls that Will said had always drawn the Darcy family to want a part of it.

They owned the building now, but only used one floor. The rest were rented out to various companies who chose a more sumptuous, old-money type, respected business front. Eliza pushed through the double doors and toward the receptionist sitting behind a large dark wood desk. "Hi, Gracie. Do you have any messages for me?"

The girl smiled. "There's a schedule change for this afternoon's meeting. Instead of two, Mr. Darcy bumped it up to eleven. Also, he says he would like to see you in his office right away."

Did he now? "Thank you, Gracie. I'll head there immediately. Anything else?"

"Just the usual email stuff. I've already sent it over to you. There's a lot, but nothing urgent."

"Thanks."

Eliza walked toward her office on the east side and snuck past Will's. His door was open a crack, but she didn't glance inside. He would have to wait a minute. She was pretty sure she'd need at least two more cups of calming herbal tea before she could face him.

She sighed as she walked into the room—it was going to be a long day. The offices were a bit larger than she was used to, mainly due to the older building's layout, but they were beautifully decorated, and the views—the views were incredible! After kicking her door shut with her foot, Eliza headed toward her overstuffed chair and sank into it. From her window, she had a front-row seat to Salt Lake City's gorgeous mountains. Nothing could be more perfect than these views—nothing. In such a challenging work environment, this was definitely a perk.

Eliza pulled her laptop forward and adjusted her chair sideways so she could continue to soak up the effects of the soothing view while she opened her account. Gracie was right—there were a lot of emails. She shook her head as she skimmed down the list. Thank goodness she had Gracie to tell her the important stuff so she didn't have to sort through it all. At least eighteen of the emails had come from Will Darcy, or his secretary.

Of *course* he would send over tons of work to prove to her that their relationship was nothing but business. She rubbed the bridge of her nose and groaned. This stress was not helping her relax. She skimmed through the last of her emails and was almost ready to close them out to be looked at later when her eye caught one dated late Friday night.

He emailed her after she turned him down?

Eliza slowly sat back up in her chair. There was absolutely no reason at all why her heart should suddenly be beating as fast as it was. She clicked on it. There was no subject line, but holy cow, it was a long email! If she printed it, it'd no doubt be three pages at least.

Elizabeth,

I've given it some thought and I'd like to say—

Knuckles wrapped on her office door. Eliza looked up and into Will's dark brown eyes. "Can I speak with you for a minute?"

No. I want to see what you had to say Friday. "I—I was just reading my emails."

"Okay, but it's urgent."

CHAPTER THREE:

Eliza pushed her computer away and sat up, motioning toward a chair across from her desk. "Have a seat, Mr. Darcy."

It wasn't until he walked closer that she saw the lines of strain on his much paler than usual face. He didn't sit— he stood behind the chair and placed one hand on it. Then he glanced around the room, as if he wished he were anywhere else but there with her.

She had never seen him this uncertain before. "What is it? Are you okay?"

He shook his head and then looked blankly at her desk.

After waiting a few seconds, she asked, "Is there something I can do?"

He ran his hands through his hair. "I don't know. Maybe. I just—I need to discuss something." Taking a deep breath, Will looked at her and then away. "Could I . . . could we . . . gah. Look, I have to go away for a bit. People are going to be asking some questions, and I—I don't know what to say or do right now. I just have to go."

Her stomach dropped. Was this because of her? He was acting very unprofessional. It just wasn't like him. How badly had she hurt him? "I'm so sorry. I had no idea you needed time away. Honestly, I feel awful about what happened Friday. Please forgive me—I should've handled the situation better. I'm sure we could—"

"Friday?" Confusion marred his features for a moment. "Oh! Yes—uh, no." Attempting a lame chuckle, he continued, "No. Uh—wow. I wish. That would be easy. Was that just this past Friday? Man, so much has happened since then. No."

Oh, my word, what happened? "Are you okay? The company? Your family?" What was going on? She knew she was probably prying more than she should, but she couldn't help it.

He held his hands out. "Um, no. Yes . . . er . . . no."

"Right." That helped so much.

Will turned toward the door. "Look, I should probably go. I just—I just wanted you to know that I won't be in for a few days and I need you to sort of cover for me, okay?"

"Wait. Why?"

He gave her a vulnerable look, as if to say, *I'm barely hanging on here. Please don't ask me anything else.*

That was it. Eliza snapped. They might not be the best of friends, but by golly, these last ten months, they'd at least been through enough to help when help was needed. He came to her for a reason, and she wasn't going to let him chicken out now. She marched to the door and shut it, then turned around with her arms folded. "You're not leaving this place until you speak actual words that make sense." She walked toward him and pointed to the chair. "Now sit. Spill. It'll be good for you to get off your shoulders."

He shook his head. "I really can't. I'm not much good at talking anyway, I'm just not, and now, so soon after finding out everything—I just can't."

She cleared her throat and leaned her hip against the mahogany desk. "You came into my office to tell me, didn't you?"

"Yes, I came here instinctively, but you and I aren't..." He finally sat down and put his elbows on his knees, his hands once again going through his hair. "I don't know what to say."

"Just start at the beginning." Eliza sat in a chair next to his. "What is this about? Is it an emergency?"

"Not what—who."

"Okay. *Who* is this about?"

"My sister."

"Your—you have a sister?" How did she not know he had a sister?

"Yes."

Eliza decided to remain silent, waiting for him to come to terms and share. After a minute or so, Will began to talk.

"She—well, my old business partner..." He trailed off.

"Yes. She was your business partner?"

"No." He sighed and straightened up. "Have you ever heard me talk about George Wickham? We called him Joe—an old football joke. Anyway, maybe you've heard me mention Joe?"

"Um, a little. Sure. So, he was your business partner?"

"Yes."

Even after being here for months she didn't know that.

"It was a long time ago—we're talking like, maybe ten years ago—back when I'd finally broken off from my dad's company and started bringing this division where it is now." He crossed his foot over a knee and stared out toward the mountain view. "Anyway, Joe was more interested in the ladies than working. Particularly ladies he could convince to give him money that he'd use on heroin, cocaine—anything he could get his hands on. I didn't realize he was a total scam artist straight away. I knew he'd get involved with stupid things—he was always excited about some shady investment or another—but I really didn't think he was bad. Not *that* bad. Even the drugs—I don't know, maybe there were signs. I just didn't see them. You know?"

When she didn't say anything, he went on. "And yeah, it wasn't good when everything came to light. I paid off somewhere like $185,000 or more in scams involving our female employees. Then, instead of going public, I paid them quietly and sent him to Spain to cool it and stave off any scandal that might get picked up by the news. We were a new company, and I couldn't handle the investment scandal it would've caused. Joe was also given explicit orders never to return to Revolutionary Innovations, or Utah, again."

"And he came back?"

Will stood up and pushed his chair in. "He didn't just come back. He somehow found my little sister—we're talking my eighteen-year-old sister!—and convinced her to elope with him."

"What?" Eliza stood up too. "Are you kidding me?"

"No. They went to Vegas, apparently, but I know he's not reckless. I know he didn't marry her—he's such a perverted monster. He probably got what he wanted out of her and then left. Or worse, got her involved in drugs and the kind of people I really don't want her around."

"How did you find out? Did she text you?"

"I haven't heard one word from her. I think he took her phone. I tried calling, and it went straight to voicemail.

"When she didn't show up Friday night, I got a little worried. By Saturday, I notified the police, but because she's eighteen, there's nothing they can do. She's an adult, and unless there's evidence of foul play, they're assuming she just took off." He sighed. "I spent the whole weekend going backwards, scouring for clues, trying to find her. When I went to her work, her boss said she'd given her two weeks' notice already and had left. So this was something that had obviously been planned and kept hidden from me for weeks!"

"I'm so sorry."

He shook his head. "Not as sorry as Joe's going to be."

"How did you find out she went to Vegas?"

"Oh, I found a tablet at the house this morning, under an armchair, where she was still signed into Facebook. The private messages floored me. I want to kill Joe. She's so naïve and has no idea about the world or men like him. None."

"When do you leave?"

"My flight leaves at one. I guess my dad had the jet in Arizona this week, so they're bringing it up here. Look, just hold down the fort until I get back, okay? I trust you. Despite everything else that went on this weekend, I just trust you. I'm not leaving Vegas until I find her. And I will find her." He fiddled with the back of the chair. "I worry most about Wickham's connections. When all the evidence was put against him last time, he had friends who dealt with sex trafficking."

She gasped. This couldn't be happening. "No!"

"Yeah, I gotta clear my head. I can't think of stuff like that. Honestly, he probably just wants in on the company— she's an heiress. At least, he thinks she is. What he doesn't know is that she can't even touch a fraction of it until she's twenty-one. And then the real stuff doesn't hit her account until she's thirty. I'm not positive he's the type of man to hang around that long—at least credibly."

"He might force her to stay with him."

"Not helping."

"Just don't go to jail, okay?"

He smirked. "Come on—are you sure you don't want to rethink that? I'd be out of your hair. Think of the peace and quiet."

She walked toward him. "It is tempting. But the thought of stopping a man like that is much more appealing. I don't think I'd be able to hold back. I'd murder him." Unconsciously, she adjusted his tie and brushed at his shoulder, straightening his suit, then realized what she had done and stopped. Shocked, her gaze met his—there was so much anger, hurt, disbelief, fear etched in him, it nearly broke her. For a few seconds, she wished they were a couple, because then she'd stand up on tiptoe and kiss some of that away and whisper the things he needed to hear. But they weren't, and she couldn't. "I'm sorry. I really, really am."

Will continued to stare right at her. Didn't he feel the tension mounting? She should totally look away, but she couldn't.

"Forgive me for this." He bent down and kissed her instead of walking away like he should, those soft lips claiming what wasn't his to claim.

When he pulled back, she was a bit breathless. My word! The man could kiss. It took every ounce of self-control she had not to grab him and kiss him again.

"Thank you for your help," he said a bit tersely as he turned away and headed toward the door. "See you at eleven."

Her trembling fingers found her mouth, and she stared at the closed door. What in the world had just happened? And why was she seeing him at eleven?

CHAPTER FOUR:

Will booked it out of Eliza's office and ducked into his, shutting the door quickly and locking it. Then he stood there, frozen, gazing blindly at his room. What was that? Seriously. What. Was. That? He cringed and closed his eyes. Any minute now, he was going to wake up and see that this whole weekend had been one long nightmare.

Starting with that stupid proposal.

He banged the back of his head lightly against the door. *Just shoot me now. Put me out of my misery.* What guy is lame enough to get up the nerve to propose to a woman who hates him and then attempt to forget about her rejection, only to kiss her the next time they meet?

Yeah, because that's exactly how to control yourself. That's how you win the girl. You scare the living daylights out of her. Wait. What? Was he trying to win the girl? No. Of course not. Never. Ugh.

He pushed away from the door and plopped onto his soft leather couch. One of these days, he was going to actually consider himself intelligent. Today wasn't that day, but eventually. Maybe. If he'd stick with what he had to do—finding his sister.

He leaned over and placed his elbows on his knees, sinking his face in his hands. Why would Georgia do this? Why would she risk everything and fall for a scam artist? At eighteen years old! That was the worst part. Sure, everyone makes mistakes . . . yadda, yadda, yadda… but not like this. Not at eighteen. And not with the worst type of cons there are!

He blamed himself completely. There was no one else, not since their mom died. Ever since then, his dad had been so busy losing himself to grief that all the responsibility of raising Georgia had fallen to Will. Not that he'd minded—he'd always loved his baby sister, and he thought they had an incredibly fun older brother/younger sister relationship. Completely open and trusting—until now. He sighed.

Since Will never spoke of the guy, Georgia had no idea Joe was such a loser. How would she know? How could she know? The man was his age, yet looked like he was in his early twenties, and was incredibly charming. Will had been too dang busy running this business and falling head over heels for the wrong woman to actually spend quality time with Georgia lately, to find out who she'd been dating.

His heart clenched in worry and fear—for the hundredth time since that morning, he felt that unfamiliar frightening pain. Was she okay? Was she safe? What had Joe done to her?

Will had been there for every special dance—helping her choose the perfect dress, taking her to whatever frivolous beauty salon she had chosen to have her makeup, nails, and hair done. And then he had rushed home from work to be there when that date arrived to guarantee this young man would treat her with respect.

She was such an incredible girl—er, young woman. Excellent grades, very musically talented, very culturally aware. She loved all forms of the arts—dancing, painting, theater, symphonies, and she was so adorably shy and sweet and kind and…

Fear became replaced with rage. It took a lot to upset Will, but Joe had certainly destroyed whatever kindness he had left. Will picked up the nearest thing he could find—some sort of ornamental piece on the coffee table—and hurled it across the room.

He jumped guiltily as it smashed into an expensive framed watercolor and broke the glass. Dang. Someone must have heard that. He quickly brushed at his hair and suit, and sure enough, his secretary knocked on his door.

"Mr. Darcy, are you all right?" she asked on the other side.

"Yes, Amy. Thank you."

"Did something break?"

"Er, yes. But it's fine. Give me a minute and I'll be out." He glanced at his watch. "On second thought, start rounding everyone up for the meeting. I'll be in the conference room in ten minutes."

As he sat back down on the couch, his fingers began to shake. Emotion so raw, so unexpected, boiled to the surface. All his life, he'd prided himself on remaining cool during any situation, not breaking, just staying firm and allowing silence to reign.

As an introvert, it was easiest not to explode in a knee-jerk reaction without first thinking everything over. He had found that his best decisions were made after spending hours away from the situation. Many business men had attempted to get him to make hasty decisions right then—and he never would. He needed time.

And he had time. Plenty of time to process how low Joe had sunk. How dare he take Will's sister! How dare he come back to Utah at all! He should be in jail, exposed for the man he was.

Will shook his head. What a fool he'd been. All along, he was convinced Joe would change if he was given another chance. It's why he kept his mouth shut and paid everyone off. But what did Joe do with that opportunity? A grown man of thirty-two targets an eighteen-year-old heiress.

Will shuddered. It was too gross even to contemplate. And was only just legal. The rage inside him boiled. Frankly, if he saw Joe right then, he would probably kill him and—

His phone rang. It was the private investigator he'd hired earlier.

"Yeah?" he asked as he got off the couch and headed toward the large window in his office.

"We've found out a bit. Not where they are yet, but it looks like we should be able to track him fairly easily just from his losing streak and the trail of casinos he's left in his wake."

Will's stomach dropped. He didn't have to look—he knew Georgia had cleaned out the family emergency money he'd placed in the safe at the house. And now it looked like Joe was having a heyday burning through that $500,000 as if it were chump change. Will didn't want to imagine how much she had personally in her savings/college fund that Joe would be able to access.

"Have you found my sister?"

"No. My initial conversations with the casino security teams haven't turned up anything so far. There are many beautiful girls in the casinos who match her description. I've sent over pictures of them both, and the casinos are scanning their high-tech recordings now. I ought to have more information for you when you land."

Will nodded. "Okay. Thanks for the update. Do you have anything else?"

"I need permission to explore other avenues, if you will."

"Anything you need to do—anything. I don't care."

The private investigator cleared his throat. "Well, this would be a bit shadier and it would cost more, but I'd like to get involved with the other side of town and start looking for her there as well."

Will closed his eyes and pinched the bridge of his nose. He really couldn't handle this right now. "Do you think he's left her on the streets? Or drugged her up and gotten her into something worse?"

"I—uh, I don't know. But gauging by the couple hundred thousand he managed to blow over the weekend, this is a man who's only thinking of himself. Hopefully she's just tucked away in some hotel room somewhere— and not actually lost."

Would Georgia know how to escape something evil like that? She was such a sweet girl, so naïve and eager to please. She could be scarred for life, especially after falling in love with him, running away to elope, and then left alone while he gambles her life away.

He never thought he'd say it, but, "Here's to weddings and hoping Joe attempted to do one thing honestly. Just long enough for me to find her, and then guarantee they divorce."

CHAPTER FIVE:

Perplexed, Eliza slowly walked over to her desk and sat down. She stared blindly out at the mountains and contemplated Will Darcy's oddness. All this time, she'd felt like he was an irritating snob. Her boss. Someone to be tolerated. It was kind of odd to consider him a normal human being with feelings, craziness in his life, stress—everything.

And then when he kissed her, when she was just thinking about kissing him—it was unreal. For that small moment, they spoke the same language—they were on the same team. For that tiniest fraction, she understood him, and it was weird. Scary. Terrifying.

And kind of nice, too.

Eliza shook her head. She honestly had no idea what was happening to her. However, she did know that if her mother ever found out she and Will had kissed, she'd never hear the end of it. The woman would begin planning their wedding. Ugh. And that *particular* thought would get Eliza nowhere.

She opened her laptop and found the email Will had sent her Friday night. In all the craziness about Will's sister, she'd forgotten.

Elizabeth,

I've given it some thought, and I'd like to say you're right. Don't get me wrong—you're not right about everything. You're just right about a few things. Mainly my character. I was a jerk to you. I've treated you unkindly, and as I tried to explain earlier, unwisely. I felt from the beginning that having you come and help the company would look like I'd failed. How am I supposed to run such a large corporation when I'm not even qualified to know what's best for it?

There you were, in all your five-foot-two no-nonsense glory, and I was mad, definitely not wanting to be in the situation I'd been forced into, and definitely not wanting to pretend to be nice to you. As far as I could tell, you were too young, too attractive, and too much trouble for your own good. You spoke out of turn, you had no concept of the way we ran things, and you continued to criticize everything that had been achieved and put into place before you came along.

"But that's what I'm paid to do!" Eliza grumbled as she looked up from the email. Of course she was going to criticize his work—it was awful! Good grief. If he'd been a perfect businessman, he wouldn't have needed an efficiency expert to begin with. In fact, most consultants were able to work part-time—but things were so bad here, she'd had to be given her own dang office!

Okay. So maybe that wasn't completely fair. It was company policy to have all the employees working full-time. She shook her head. How many hours a day had she muttered over the absurdity of having to stay there all day long when she didn't really need to? And she definitely didn't need a posh office. She shrugged. Granted, when she joined, sales went up even higher than the billion-dollar company could've imagined. When you're playing in the big leagues, a 22% increase is nothing to sneer at. In fact, Will was certain this increase happened because she was there all day long and could continually oversee each department.

Within six weeks, their offices had begun to see an improvement, and within six months, there was talk of keeping her on permanently. Ha! Wild hogs could fly to Britain, and she still wouldn't stay here a second longer than her eighteen-month contract. However, that had nothing to do with Will's odd confessional. Curious, Eliza slipped off her heels, leaned back, and began to read again.

Yes, we argued a lot. It's something I came to respect about you—that you wouldn't take trash from me. You'd give it back, sometimes hurtling the junk at my face, but always giving back. I loved that you weren't afraid of me, like so many people are. You were smart, sharp, and just exactly what this company needed.

I admit, there were days when I wondered if I'd gotten under your skin and actually hurt you during our arguments. You have such a hard shell, I guess I'd convinced myself that you were fine and business was business. But I see now that I was wrong. And I'm sorry. Honestly, it really worries me that I made you believe we were enemies, that my childish actions caused you to doubt yourself and your worth (and don't say they didn't!) so much that you were confused when I proposed.

She snorted at that last part. That man's ego could topple the Eiffel Tower.

Well, honestly, I was confused too. I'd bought a ring on impulse about a week ago, and then on another whim, I found myself at your door tonight. Seriously, the words were out before I had a minute to realize what I was saying. And then you were angry, and it was just fail. From the moment I showed up at your door, it was all fail. You're right. I don't know you. I don't know anything about you, really. I mean, I thought I did. I thought being so close to you all year had shown me so much, but it didn't show me this side.

What? The side where you get told no?

In my defense, I've never proposed before, and—

Eliza sat up. "Shut it!" Her hand went to her mouth. Of course he hadn't proposed before. He'd be married if he had. Who'd turn him down? No one.

But why pick her? Out of all of Salt Lake, or anywhere in the world, really... why her? She knew he'd answered her, but she wasn't buying it. There had to be something deeper there—but what? She was completely flabbergasted.

Just then, her phone rang, causing her to jump and nearly knock the laptop off the desk. "Hello?"

"Eliza?" her mom asked.

She rubbed her nose, trying to alleviate her stress, and leaned back in the chair. "Yep, it's me. Are you okay? What's up?"

"I know you're at work and super busy, but I wanted to tell you that I heard from my neighbor that Will Darcy is heading to Las Vegas today, and I was wondering if you—"

"Wait. Wait. What? How does Patty know that Will's going to Vegas?"

"Oh, so he *is*?" She giggled.

"I didn't say that!" Eliza groaned.

"But you didn't say he wasn't, which means he is! I can't wait to tell her she's right."

"Mom, seriously. Stop. Where do you guys get your information, anyway?" Eliza was pretty sure they could give the CIA a run for their money. "And why does it matter where Will goes?"

"Because if he'll be there, then we're going to Vegas for my birthday this weekend!"
   "What?"

CHAPTER SIX:

"Mom, I refuse to go with you to Las Vegas just to track down my boss. No way. No how. Never."

"Excuse me, Elizabeth Bennet, you will most certainly take me to Vegas—like you promised—for my birthday—"

"I didn't promise I'd take you there!" Eliza was sounding desperate. She began to flip through her computer to make sure she could clear her schedule, knowing perfectly well she'd never win this battle. The guilt her mom would lay on her was too real.

"You promised to take me anywhere I asked to go because you forgot my birthday last year. Don't you remember?"

How could she forget? It was quickly turning into the worst mistake of her life. She sighed. "Yes, Mom. I remember." It looked like she had a couple of meetings on Friday afternoon, but nothing that couldn't be changed.

"Good. And you'll be wearing this adorable dress I found at Macy's the other day."

"You bought me a dress?" *This should be an adventure.*

"No. Not yet. But I'll be shopping this afternoon with Patty since you and I are going to Vegas, and I'll bring home that dress for you."

Great. The last thing she needed was some sequined number. "No, Mom. Don't. This is your birthday, remember? I have plenty of clothes. I'll be fine. This trip wouldn't be about me anyway. It'd be all about you."

"Oh, heckfire it ain't!" Her mom was clearly beginning to lose it. "You'd better believe that if my daughter brings home Mr. Darcy from Las Vegas as my future son-in-law, I'd be over the moon!"

Eliza laughed. She had to, because crying about this wasn't an option. "You're crazy, Mom."

"I'm not. I just know a good opportunity when I see it. And you'd better believe this trip will be one of the best birthday presents you could ever give me."

"I have no doubt." She rolled her eyes. "But can you promise me one thing? Drop the Will Darcy drama. I don't need this right now. I'm busy, and I have *no* plans to marry him."

"Yet." She could imagine her mom's grin.

"Good-bye. We'll talk about this later. I love you."

"Bye." Her mom giggled again as the phone clicked off.

Eliza groaned, and then heard a soft tap on the outside of her door. "Come in." It was Gracie. "Oh, hi. How can I help you?" From the looks of it, Gracie had been standing there for some time and had probably heard a bunch of that conversation.

Nice.

"Uh, Mr. Darcy sent me over to see if you still planned on making the meeting."

"Was that now?" She glanced at her watch. Sure enough, she was late. "Yes, let him know I'll be there in just a second."

While the secretary left, Eliza scrambled to slip her shoes back on and grabbed her leather-bound notebook. As she headed down the hall toward the conference room, she noticed the whole place was empty. Everyone was in that meeting except her, of course. Way to show efficiency. She had never been late before.

"Sorry," she whispered as she nipped into the room and sat down.

"Important call?" Will asked. Fifteen sets of eyes looked right at her.

Eliza could feel a blush forming. How did he know? "Family issues," she sputtered out lamely. She never should've picked up the phone. He caught her eye as if trying to read her. In answer, her face grew even redder. *Now he's really going to think something's up. This has got to stop.*

She cleared her throat. "So, what have I missed?"

Will went back to business. "I was just letting everyone know I've had an emergency come up with the division in Vegas and will be there indefinitely until we get everything sorted out."

She nodded.

"I've also informed them that any emergencies here will be settled by you and Charles Bingley."

Charles, the VIP, interrupted. "Actually, turn them over to Eliza for now. She'll come to me if anything's too urgent. I'm still catching up with the New York building and work crews out there."

For the past two months, Charles had been flying back and forth to New York, working with the crews and hiring the task force that would be the Revolutionary Innovations team in the Big Apple. They'd had branches across the country with buildings in Michigan, Massachusetts, and Connecticut, but now they had decided to expand again, and expand quickly.

The Darcy empire had most definitely proven itself worthy enough to be completely established in New York. However, that meant with Charles gone and Will away, the bulk of the work would be left in her lap.

"Is that okay?" Will asked. "You will definitely be compensated for your time."

Did she have a choice? "Yes. It's fine. I'll field all the typical issues, unless there's something I can't handle on my own. I'll try not to disturb Mr. Bingley."

"Sorry to do this to you, Eliza," Charles said as he gave a rueful look. He was an awesome guy—just super nice. He'd even taken her sister, Jane, out on a few dates, but ever since this New York building construction began, it'd taken up all of his extra time, and so he'd backed way off. At least, that's what she reminded herself whenever she thought of Jane's heartbreak over Charles suddenly putting work first.

"No worries." She smiled. What's the worst that could happen, anyway?

The discussion brought up a few more concerns, which were handled briefly before they disbanded. Will caught up with her on their way back down the hall.

"So, are you sure you're okay with me leaving you in charge?" he asked. "You seemed a little flustered back there."

"Did I? Again, I apologize for arriving late."

"Is everything all right with your family?"

"Yep." She smiled a bit and decided to change the subject. "Well, I hope everything works out in Vegas."

They stopped at her door. "Me too." For a small moment, he let his guard down and allowed the stress to show. He touched her arm. "I know the timing is off, and I'm sorry to be dumping everything on you like this, but thank you. Just thank you." He took a deep breath and nodded. "I'm not even worried. I know you'll do fine running the show."

She shrugged. Honestly, she wasn't that worried either. "Everything will be fine. You go save the world."

His dark brown eyes softened. "I'll save it while you run it."

She would've chuckled at his attempt at a joke, but that look in his eyes was too hypnotizing.

"It's good to have you on board with us. You have no idea what it means to be able to leave like this and focus one hundred percent on finding my sister."

They were now a team. This unity was unlike anything she'd ever experienced before. "I'm happy to help."

"Thanks. Eliza, I wish…" He trailed off.

She looked away. "Go. Bring her home. And then we'll celebrate." Of course she meant *everyone* would celebrate, but hadn't realized how awkward it sounded until after it was said. It didn't matter—Will wasn't paying attention.

"Right. I'll keep in touch. Let's have a quick daily phone meeting, okay?"

"Good idea." Then she could keep him up-to-date on all the issues, and still be able to pry a bit to satisfy her curiosity about his sister. "Text me once you figure out a time, and I'll carve it out for you."

"Okay."

Good-bye. Neither of them said it. She almost didn't want him to. There was something so significant happening that she really couldn't think straight. But it *was* a teensy bit exciting and a ton uncomfortable and more confusing than anything.

His gaze dropped to her lips, and she lightly gasped.

Would he kiss her again? *No. He'd better not—I mean, he'd better do it. No, wait. Not do it.*

"Mr. Darcy?" his secretary called from behind, breaking the odd spell. "Your plane arrived early and is ready to leave whenever you are."

"Thanks."

Then he was gone. Didn't say good-bye—just turned and focused on the tasks he should be focused on. And when he walked out of that building, she was surprised to find that he'd taken a tiny piece of her heart with him.

CHAPTER SEVEN:

"So Mom says you guys are going to Las Vegas without me," Jane joked from across the table at their favorite Mexican restaurant.

"Yeah, Mom says a lot of things I'm not sure about right now." Eliza took another bite of her salad.

Jane laughed. "So glad it's you and not me."

"Ha! You know that if she could find a way to get you to New York to spy on Charles, she'd do it."

Jane nearly spit out her drink. "Don't give her any ideas!" She laughed. "Besides, you're crazy if you think spying is all she'd have me do."

"You're right. Can you imagine the humiliation when you just 'happen' to be at the same place he is?"

She rolled her eyes. "With *Mom*."

Chuckling, Eliza took another bite of the yummy salad. After swallowing, she said, "Come on—it wouldn't be that bad. I'm sure of it."

Jane gave her the "look" before biting into her own salad.

"Just think. If Mom had her way, we'd both be married to Revolutionary Innovations," Eliza said.

Jane snorted. "Yeah, nothing like being married to your work!"

Eliza set her fork down and placed an elbow on the table. "You know, it wouldn't be a bad place for you to work. The environment is good. Have you ever thought about it?"

"About what?" Jane's eyes were huge. "Working for Charles Bingley? *Are you out of your mind?*"

She shrugged. "I don't know. It'd be a good fit for you."

Her sister shook her head. "No way. I'm not about to give up my cushy job as a school librarian now that I've finally made it there."

Jane really was unbelievably amazing. With her level of genius, she could've had any job she wanted—she'd received offers to train and teach people all over the world. But when their Aunt Phyllis needed a substitute for the elementary school librarian, Jane jumped at the chance to help family out. There were several older teachers who applied for the position, but none with the knowledge Jane had of the new computer system the school district was setting up. So, as the principal, Aunt Phyllis came to her niece first.

"Do you ever worry you're wasting your life away?" Eliza asked her cautiously.

Jane seemed surprised. "No. Why?"

She shrugged. "I don't know—just wondered. Curious, I guess. There are days when I definitely envy you."

"I kind of really love my job. Sure, I'm not making much money, but the ability to inspire kids to read and get them excited about it—that changes the dynamics of everything. I could be making a ton of money for myself, and maybe I will one day. But for now, I love the idea that for every kid who gets excited about reading, I've changed their life. I've made them happier, smarter, more confident, and more imaginative. They now can read about many other people who change their own worlds—whether fictional or real, it doesn't matter. They're given hope and advice and wisdom just by opening a book… and I'm totally rambling now, aren't I?" She blushed.

Eliza laughed. "It's the good kind of rambling. Shows what a great heart you have." She took a bite and chewed. "And just between you and me, Charles Bingley is a fool."

"Eliza!"

"What? He is. Any man who would give up you for more work is insane. The end."

Jane looked at her for a moment. "Thanks. Though, I have to say, I'm curious to meet the man who'll be brave enough to propose to you one day. I can't wait to see you knocked off your feet by someone."

Eliza looked down and cleared her throat. She tapped her mouth with her napkin and stared at her food, swirling it around with her fork.

"What is it?" Jane asked. "Come on—out with it. There's a guy, isn't there?"

When Eliza looked up, her sister's eyes were all sparkly with mischief. Time to nip this in the bud. "There is most definitely *not* a guy. At least, I don't think so. I'm certainly not in love with him."

"Okay." Jane took a bite and chewed. "But…?"

"But what?"

"But …?" Jane insisted.

Eliza took a deep breath and expelled it, then said quickly, "Will Darcy proposed."

Jane dropped her fork. It clattered loudly on the plate below. "What did you say?"

"You heard me." Eliza looked at the fork and then the hand that was frozen in midair. "You dropped your fork."

Her sister's voice rose. "I'm sorry. Did you say William Darcy *proposed* to you?"

"Yes!" Eliza hissed. "Now be quiet. And don't you *dare* tell Mom!"

Jane slowly became awake and folded her arms. "How am I supposed to be quiet with news like that? Good grief, Elizabeth! When were you planning on telling people you two are getting married? Or even better yet, when were you going to announce that you actually liked him?"

Eliza leaned over her plate and whispered frantically, "We are not getting married. I told him no. I can't stand him. That's what makes this whole thing so weird."

"Oh. My. Gosh." Jane's jaw dropped.

"Yeah, I know."

"Oh. My. Gosh."

"Yeah, *I know*. You can stop now."

"Oh. My. G—"

"Seriously, stop." She held up her hands. "Yes. I turned him down. Yes, he's totally hot and amazing and like, a billionaire, or whatever. Yes, I know. Yes, he was upset. Yes, I was shocked. No, I don't want to talk about it. And I swear down that if Mom ever hears One. Single. Word. Of. This, you're dead. You got that? D.E.A.D."

Jane crossed her heart with her finger. "I promise on my Anne of Green Gables collection that I won't tell a soul you completely destroyed Salt Lake City's most eligible bachelor. And possibly the hottest man in all of America."

Eliza would've banged her head on the table, but there was food on it. Instead, she whined—what else was she supposed to do when her big sister put stuff that way? "I'm sure he isn't the hottest guy in America."

"Really?" Jane was on a roll. "Who helped fund the new women's shelter last month? As in, literally dropped the 7.8 million needed to complete the fundraising and allow them to begin construction immediately instead of in two years? Hmm?"

"Er, was it Will?"

"And whose generous support of Operation Underground Railroad allowed the whole organization to be fully functional for over a year while they saved kids around the world from sex slavery?"

Eliza's heart dropped. "You're kidding. That was *him*?"

"And who donates more to cancer treatments and cures than any of the other charitable donations given in Utah combined?"

"Shut it. Don't. I'll start falling in love with him if you keep this up." Eliza pushed her plate away. "You know how much I love OUR, and how many 5Ks I've run and organized for cancer fundraising ever since Dad got diagnosed."

"And I know you and women's shelters too." Jane crossed her heart again, and then zipped her lips. "I promise, no one will know you shattered Salt Lake City's biggest superhero."

"Jane!"

Her sister took a deep breath, and it was crazy. For a moment, it looked like tears had begun to form. "Honestly, though, I can see why he chose you."

"I don't want to think about it right now."

"You don't have to. You don't ever have to think about it again because frankly, if you're not in love with him, it's okay. This is your choice. Your life. But tonight, when you look in the mirror and feel a little smaller than normal, know this one thing—*I love you*." She grinned a lopsided grin. "I love you. And even if you don't understand yet why he'd fall for you, I get it. You two just match. Perfectly."

CHAPTER EIGHT:

Later that night, Jane was right. Eliza did feel a little bit smaller than she had earlier. After tidying up the kitchen and living room to the hum of the T.V. news station in the background, she curled up on her white sofa and tucked an afghan under her feet. Her thoughts wandered all over the new Mr. Darcy. Everything she learned about him seemed to shatter the old ideas she had of him. Caring, protective brother, a fair business partner, and now Mr. Charity—on top of his good looks, wealth, and charm that made that incredible man.

She wrapped her arms around her legs and set her chin on her knees. In fact, she felt extremely small and unimportant when compared to his much larger contributions to society. Sure, she raised a few hundred dollars with each fun run, but how could she even compete with the money and generosity of such a man? Why would any organization even need her?

In a huff, she tossed the blanket aside and stood up. Flipping on the light in the bathroom, she examined herself. Almost thirty, and too stubborn to see her own worth. She faced her green eyes head on and really searched for what others saw. That drive. That fire. That innate ability to be right. Her own silly pride. And then it hit her! She wasn't feeling worthless because of Will's importance.

No, she was feeling so small because maybe—just maybe— she had judged him wrong, and she wasn't quite certain what to do with that knowledge.

If she had been wrong about him, and if he really was someone she should've taken time to get to know better, the joke was on her. The loss was hers, and not his. And if she had wrongly judged him, how many other people out there had been cast aside by her selfishness and unkind thoughts?

Tonight was not a good night. Those times of deep reflection, while character building and cleansing, are very painful. She blinked back a few tears for her stupidity and callousness, no doubt being way harder on herself than she needed to be. But it was a good moment of change. And if she understood anything, it was that change meant growth, and growth was always good.

She wiped the last tear and started washing her face, but then she heard her phone ring. She washed as fast as she could and then patted herself dry.

By the time she got to the phone, they'd already hung up. Glancing at it, she saw there were two unread texts and the missed call. The texts were from her mom, but the call was from Will. Curious, she collected the blanket again and sat down on the couch, this time reaching for her remote and turning off the TV.

She stared at the phone as she contemplated the excited sparks surging through her. Then, waiting a minute longer so she wouldn't seem too eager, she finally gave in and returned the call.

"Hello?" his deep voice answered on the second ring.

"Hi. Sorry I missed you."

"How was everything today?"

How many times had they spoken before? How many times had they discussed office concerns, and this time—

this time she could almost imagine there being more. That tension between them of wanting to say more, but not being able to.

"I—it was good," she stumbled a bit. "How was your flight? Did you make it okay?"

"Yeah." His warm response wrapped her up in tingles. "It was a nice flight." He laughed softly. "Not that it wouldn't be, with the private ride and all."

See? There it was, his snobbishness coming off again. "Of course." She felt her heart cool and straightened her legs. "Well, great. Glad everything went okay. So, have you heard any news about Georgia?"

"No. Well, a little. I was given a list of hotels where her credit cards had been used."

She growled. "I seriously would think about murdering the man."

"It's a possibility." He sounded tired. "I mean, jail time wouldn't be too bad, knowing Joe wasn't going around scamming anyone else."

"Nah, they wouldn't put you behind bars. You're too pretty." She yawned.

"Ha. Do you really think so?"

She rolled her eyes. "Yep. You're quite the fisherman, aren't you?"

"Hey, I'll take any bait I can get from the one girl who hates my guts."

"Whatever. I don't hate your guts."

He snorted, a very manly guffaw. "Whatever makes you sleep better at night, princess."

She sat up. "Hey! I resent that remark."

"You mean you act just like one, right?"

"You're so lucky there's a state between us. You know darn well I'm the least like a princess of any girl you've met."

He chuckled. "And what does that mean?"

"As if I needed pampering, and a man to look after me, and all that nonsense that says I can't look after myself."

"Let me see. Demanding, arrogant, prideful, condescending, self-righteous, and beautiful. Yep, that about sums it up. You're a princess in my book."

She gasped. Really, tonight was not the night for this. "Of all the things to say to me! As if I'm half of that. Good grief." And people wonder why women were the superior sex.

Laughing, he interrupted. "I'm just kidding, and you know it."

Did she? "Sure, make excuses now." She tried not to let it affect her, but his words hit a little too close to home.

He sighed. "Look, I'm sorry. My tongue is quicker than my brain sometimes. Forgive me?"

"Yeah, don't worry about it. I'm tough as nails, remember?"

She knew that groan—he was wincing. "I'm one of those Neanderthal men who need a lot of practice interacting with women."

"Ha! Said the most wanted guy in Salt Lake. I'm not buying it. You've had plenty of practice."

His voice got softer. "You're right. But now that it matters, I seem to get everything wrong."

Eliza felt her heart skip a beat as Will cleared his throat.

"Well, I guess I'd better leave you to it. How does this time tomorrow work for you? Is it too late? Too early?"

She glanced at the clock. "Nine works."

"Okay. Let's catch up tomorrow at nine, then."

"Perfect."

"Oh, and Eliza?"

"Yeah?"

He paused a moment. "Do you . . . have you . . . I mean, by any chance, have you read the email I sent Friday night?"

"I, uh…" Did she finish it? In all that day's confusion, she wasn't certain. "I started it, but I don't think I've read it all the way through. Why?"

"Good!" He sighed with relief. "Do me a favor— don't."

CHAPTER NINE:

"What? Why?" Eliza asked.

Will sounded a bit desperate. "Just trust me. You can read the whole email later—well, when I say. Just promise me you won't yet."

Now she had to know what it said. "Are you kidding me, Will?"

"No. No, I'm not. I'm dead serious."

"But now I want to read it."

"I know, but please don't."

This made no sense. "But what if I already had? Then what?"

"Then I'm pretty sure we wouldn't be talking like this. Just do me a favor and stop thinking about it for a few weeks. Okay? Just give me a little while to prove it."

My word, she was going to die of curiosity now. "Prove what?"

"It."

She groaned. "You're the worst."

"Yeah, yeah, I know. So you've told me."

"You're the most annoying man ever."

"So does that mean you won't read it?"

She grunted. "Yes. Though you owe me."

"Thank you. Whatever you think I should do to repay you will be worth it."

"Gah. Stop. You're making it worse."

He chuckled. "Sorry. But it is kind of fun."

"Will…"

"Yes?"

"I'll talk to you tomorrow." She grinned, though she certainly wasn't trying to.

"Goodnight, princess."

"Ugh!" But he didn't hear—the phone had cut off. The wimp. If he'd been in the same room, she would've tossed something at his head. Or punched him in the arm. Or kicked his butt. Or kissed that stupid grin off his face—Wait. What?

She closed her eyes. Yeah, she was a lot more tired than she realized. Instead of having imaginary conversations with the dork, she took the afghan with her and climbed into bed, determined—but not quite succeeding—not to dream about a handsome, dark-haired, conceited moron who was driving her nuts.

***

Will put his phone down and froze on the overstuffed chair in his hotel suite. Counting to ten, he finally exhaled and opened his eyes. His heart pounded harder than it had on Friday night, and that was really saying something. He clenched his right fist and then released it, begging the tension in his body to fade at the same time.

If he didn't know any better, he'd say he was close to giddy, a feeling he'd never experienced in his whole life. What was it about that irritating woman that drove him over the edge like this? Never had he felt so lost and unsure of himself or as seriously stupid as he did around her.

But that voice!

He shivered as flashes of remembrance ran through him. Her warm, raspberry-kissed voice had caused him to fall in love with her months ago, but to listen to it amplified like that, to hear her soft, sultry tones prick their way into his eardrums and down his neck caused major chaos inside him.

Who was he kidding? He was a wreck! One nightmarish wreck. And he had been since the moment she walked into his office a year ago. He groaned and rubbed his eyes.

He was also tired, very tired. But the night was still young. In fact, in Las Vegas, it was just beginning. After glancing at his watch, he picked up his phone and slipped it into his jeans pocket. The standard for meeting these men would've probably warranted a suit and tie, but not tonight. Not now. He wanted to draw the least amount of attention to himself as possible. Instead, he opted for a crisp black button-up shirt and some designer jeans, with casual footwear. Something that showed young, playful, money. Nothing that would stand out.

With ten minutes to spare, he walked out of his hotel room and down the long hallway to the elevator. When he headed into the smoked-filled lounge full of people in glittering mayhem, he could see the P.I. already waiting for him. They'd be meeting the undercover police chief and an elite collection of casino owners at the lounge's private bar. None of them would be drinking—they had some intense business to conduct, and he insisted that his paycheck was worth fully sober men who treated this matter as seriously as he did.

He took another deep breath, pushing out all thoughts of Elizabeth Bennet, and focused on the task at hand. No matter what it took, he would not leave Vegas without his little sister. And heaven help anyone who tried to stop him.

***

Two days later, Eliza still hadn't managed to get the man out of her head. It certainly didn't help that her mom was constantly talking about their Vegas trip. The Vegas trip she had yet to tell Will about. It was already Wednesday, and they would be there Friday night once the office closed. At this rate, she might as well surprise him. Then again, she didn't have to follow him around.

Las Vegas was a big city, and there was no way of knowing if they'd be in the same lounge at the same time. When he called, she'd ask where he was going to be, and then she'd keep her mom away from him. She grinned. It sounded brilliant. She was certain Will wouldn't survive meeting her mother. Or even worse—how would Eliza survive the two of them meeting?

She shuddered as she headed out of the office.

The day had been pretty good. Only a small hiccup over at the plant that manufactured some of their home products, but that was an easy fix. Just a short phone call to the general manager, and ten minutes later, feathers were unruffled and they were back in production. It amazed her how so many times, one small detail would get misunderstood and everything would come to a standstill. Nothing major. Certainly nothing to stop manufacturing over, but whatever it was, people would allow it to build up until someone freaked out and business halted until the misunderstanding could be fixed.

She smiled ruefully as she pushed through the main doors and stepped into the beautiful May sunshine. It kind of reminded her of relationships in general. They would go along fine until some small thing would pause everything and then—wham. Ruffled feathers and all that nonsense over a little misunderstanding.

"Hey, Eliza, wait up!"

She turned to find Charles Bingley heading out of the building on the ramp toward the company parking garage. "Is everything okay?"

He lightly jogged to catch up. His blond hair still looked perfect when he stopped. It so wasn't fair. If she'd just run like that, her mop would've been a huge mess of flyaways and wispies.

Grinning, he nodded his head. "Yeah, everything is fine. I was actually hoping to catch you alone—you know, away from the office. Would you like to grab a quick bite to eat so we can talk? I need to ask you something about your sister."

CHAPTER TEN:

They'd been sitting at the table for twelve minutes, and Charles still hadn't mentioned Jane once. Instead, he was still staring at his menu. She thought not reading the rest of Will's email was going to kill her—nah, this curiosity was much worse. What would Jane's sort-of-ex want to talk about, anyway? He'd made it clear he had no time for her a couple of months ago, so was he having a change of heart?

Chicken Alfredo with Caesar salad. There. Done. Easy. It's not like it's hard to choose Italian food, was it? The waiter brought over some breadsticks, and Eliza chewed on one.

"Do you need a minute more to decide?" the girl asked him.

Charles looked up. "Uh, yeah, just a couple. Sorry."

"No worries. I'll be back when you're ready."

Eliza smiled at the waitress and then took another bite of bread. She tried desperately not to drum her nails on the table. Showing impatience wasn't exactly the way to get someone to spill their secrets. But honestly, what else was she supposed to do?

She studied the top of his hipster-parted hair and wondered for the eightieth time what he wanted to talk about.

It had been the end of February when her sister knocked on her door and planted herself on the couch. The tears didn't take long to come. Eliza knew they'd only been dating for a few months, but Jane honestly thought they'd stick it out. Part of her figured Charles was *the one*.

Eliza had held her sister and rationalized everything as best she could, but it wasn't enough. Jane had fallen for him, and he clearly didn't reciprocate. Eliza didn't blame Jane for being confused. It wasn't like Charles hid anything. My goodness, he gushed about this gorgeous girl he was dating to anyone who'd listen. And then, bam—it was over. Just like that. He was going to be too busy in New York, so they had to end things. Not even willing to try it out, or do the long-distance thing, or anything. Just, sorry.

It was awful. And odd.

And Jane was too kind to ask him about it, to call him out and put him on the spot and make him explain what had really happened. Instead, she wiped her tears, shrugged her shoulders, and said that if he ever felt the need to explain it to her, he would. Until then, she was a big girl, and over was over. It hurt, but it was what it was.

Eliza had to go back to work and sporadically interact with him, and Jane rarely brought him up. And life went on.

Until today.

As soon as they'd both placed their orders and the waitress left, Eliza pounced. She honestly couldn't wait another moment. "So, what would you like to know about Jane?" *Come on—spit it out.*

He looked at her in surprise, and then a shy dimple peeked out on his left cheek. "I don't know. I mean, I do. I have a few things I'd like to know, but I don't really know how to ask."

"Well, how about you start at the beginning?"

He picked up a breadstick and twirled it around. "Can I ask if Will mentioned anything to you?"

Will? "About what?"

"Er, nothing. I was just wondering if you two had ever talked about me and your sister."

She scrunched her brow and thought back. "Not that I can remember. Why? Did he ever say anything to you? Did he find it weird or something?"

"Uh…" He looked up and evaded the question. "How is Jane, anyway? She keeping busy at the school?"

"Yep." Okay, what in the world was he hiding? "Kids and teachers and parents love her."

He grinned, that dimple peeping out again. "Good. I loved watching her around the kids. She's really amazing, isn't she?"

Heck with it. If he thought she was amazing, then— "Why did you break up with her?"

His eyebrows rose. "Did we break up? Is that how she saw it?"

Eliza glanced away, not sure how to respond. "Uh, yeah. What else would you call it when the guy says he doesn't have time for you anymore?"

He winced. "Okay, that hurt. Did it really come off that callous?"

She pulled out her phone and set it on the table. "Why don't you ask her?"

Charles ran his fingers through his hair, messing it up for the first time that day. "See, that's what I don't get. It shouldn't matter, right? Like, me saying we needed to take a break—that shouldn't have hurt her."

Was he insane? "Why would you say that?"

He blinked. "Well, because she didn't really like me.'"

Eliza was so confused. "Are we still talking about Jane Bennet? My sister?"

"Yes . . ." Now he looked out of it.

She chuckled. "Okay, so we seemed to have some wires crossed here. Let's start at the easiest place to unravel. Why would you think my sister didn't like you?"

"Well, it was obvious."

Eliza's jaw dropped. "To who? Far as I could tell, she was totally into you. And actually, since she's my sister and confides in me constantly, I'm going to go with . . . you're wrong."

"But I was told that she didn't. . ." His voice trailed off, and she zeroed in.

"Who would say something like—" She gasped. Her gaze collided with his. "It was Will, wasn't it?"

He leaned back in his chair and tossed his uneaten breadstick back in the basket. "See, I knew you'd been talking about us. All that time, I was completely falling for her, and Will was right. She was only after me because I was at Revolutionary Innovations. The little gold digger didn't even like me."

Eliza would've spit water all over the guy if she'd been drinking "Wait a minute. Let me get this straight—no, hang on. First, let's get *this* straight. No matter what you heard from your friend, *William Darcy*, I know for a fact, he's wrong." She raised her hands up in a "don't shoot" gesture. "I know, I know, as hard as it is to believe the man could be wrong at all, he is. Was. So is. Constantly." How she wished he was here so she could give him a piece of her mind.

"Second . . ." She held up two fingers. "My sister has never been and never will be a gold digger. Do you understand? *Never.* That woman has more intelligence in her body than you do in your pinky toe. The little gross one. Actually, the fungus-covered pinky toe." Ugh. "Wait. Maybe I got that backwards. Maybe she has more intelligence in her toe than you do in your—gah! You know what I mean." The rage that was building inside her made it too difficult to speak. "She's never needed your money, or anyone else's. If she wanted it, she'd make her own!"

"So I was wrong?" He looked a little pale. Served him right.

"And third, yes," she whispered. "She liked you. A lot. A whole lot more than you liked her, obviously. And you know what else?"

He shook his head as a flash of pain slashed through his eyes.

"Despite whatever your stupid *friend* thinks, it isn't that she doesn't deserve you—No! *You* don't deserve *her*." She stood up to go. If she didn't leave right then, she'd burst into furious, horrid tears.

As she headed out of the restaurant, she punched numbers into her cell.

"Mom, unpack your suitcase. We're not going to Vegas."

"What? Why?"

"Because I don't look good in orange!"

"What does that mean?"

"That means the next time I see *Mr. Darcy*, he's dead."

CHAPTER ELEVEN:

Eliza's mom had been relentless on the phone the whole drive home, demanding to know what was going on, but she just didn't feel like telling her. Not yet. "We'll talk about this later. I need to process first."

"But I'm afraid you might be overreacting. I mean, putting off our plans for my birthday seems a little rash—don't you think?"

"Possibly. But I'd rather not contemplate it right now. I'm just not in the mood to discuss. So please, let's drop it." Besides, if anyone deserved to know what was going on first, it was Jane. And she just couldn't bring herself to tell her yet.

"I don't know what happened, or what Will Darcy did, but if you just talked to him, I'm sure things would work out."

"I love you, Mom. I can't do this right now. Please trust me. Good-bye. We'll talk later."

"Fine. Goodnight, dear." Her mom clicked off the phone.

For some reason, Eliza felt even worse than before. She chucked her purse onto the coffee table as she walked through the door and plopped down on the couch. It wasn't fair for her mom to be thrown in the middle of all this. However, there was no way Eliza could be that close to Will and not go off on him.

She needed to approach him when she was rational. Once she had time to think.

Slipping off her shoes, she curled her feet under her and grabbed the nearest accent pillow. Poor Jane. Who would ever believe that about her? Who could? And what right did Will have, poking his nose into their relationship anyway?

The words she'd like to call him right now would make a sailor blush. She punched the pillow and lay down on it. This was awful. Everything had begun to look up, and now, now she couldn't even think about him without getting mad.

It's a good thing she turned him down! She couldn't believe he'd had the audacity to ask her to marry him—her, the sister of a gold digger. Ha. What a hard dilemma he must have faced, since of course he knew what other members of her family were like.

It was so humiliating that he'd think that of Jane, let alone sharing his idiotic thoughts with the guy Jane liked. Why didn't he come to Eliza first? She would've set him straight in a heartbeat. But to break them up? Seriously? Because he didn't think they were right together? And he didn't believe Jane liked Charles. This was such a ridiculous junior high school mentality, she could scream. Why were grown adults allowed to act this way?

She'd fallen asleep. She must have, because the next thing she remembered was hearing the phone ring. In a daze, she frantically turned the living room upside down, only to realize it was in her purse.

It was Will, of course.

She sighed and set the phone on the floor while she curled back on the couch. Was it really only nine? It felt like eleven.

A few seconds later, the phone rang again.

The screen lit with Will Darcy's name. By the third time, she turned her phone off completely.

Nope. Not tonight. She made her way into bed and crashed. Some things were just better dealt with in the morning.

When Eliza woke the next day, there were two voicemails from Will. She wondered if Charles had called him last night and so he was attempting to make some sort of amends. Good. He should be groveling right now. She pattered into the kitchen and pulled out a leftover salad. Nothing tasted better to her than vegetables first thing in the morning. As weird as it might seem, salad was her favorite meal for breakfast. Eliza had noticed years ago that it'd keep her more energized throughout the day if she actually ate what other people usually ate for lunch and dinner. She typically kept cereal and yogurt on hand for dessert.

Once she was all set up, she called her voicemail, just in case she was mistaken and this was something urgent.

It was.

"Hey, Eliza, I don't know if anything's wrong on your end, but I hope you're okay. I've called quite a few times, so now I'm just going to pop this into voicemail. We found my sister. I still haven't located Joe yet, but Georgia's pretty shaken up. She's with me in my suite, and she'd really like to have some of her own clothes to wear and a few other items. Apparently, he sold her suitcase too, and she really doesn't feel like shopping for new stuff. I'd fly up and get them, but I'm afraid to leave her, honestly. Not that I think she'd run away or something—I'm just…" The phone beeped. Voicemail must've ended.

Oh, my gosh! He'd found her! For a minute, Eliza forgot all her troubles as the reality of his words sank in and a huge wave of relief washed over her.

The next voicemail came on:

"Sorry, I guess that message was too long. So, like I was saying, I think Georgia is going through some PTSD, or something. So, I have a huge favor to ask—would you mind calling me back as soon as possible so this voicemail doesn't go off again while I'm asking you? Thanks. You're the best. Bye."

Having worked with the man for over a year, she knew what he was going to ask before she called him. He needed her to fly out there with stuff for Georgia. And as much as she was trying to be mad at him right now, there was a very upset girl who needed help, and that tugged upon her heartstrings much more firmly than the irritation she felt for Will.

Glancing at the time and seeing that it was seven a.m., she called him back.

"Hello?" he answered groggily.

"Hey. Late night?" she asked.

He muttered something and then said, "Yeah. I'm glad you called. I was beginning to worry."

She could hear him yawn as she put her tea kettle on the stove. "Afraid I'd gotten mugged?"

"Something like that." He cleared his throat. "So, I've got a favor to ask you."

"Yep. I know," she said as she placed an herbal tea bag into her favorite mug. "You'd like me to bring Georgia's stuff."

"Oh, would you?" He sounded relieved.

"I'm thinking about it."

"I'd need you to stop by the house and collect it for her. I could email you the list. It's not much."

"Why don't you bring her home?"

"I tried." He sighed. "Apparently, she wants to stay here with me and watch Joe go down. Not that I blame her. So, are you okay with helping?"

She took a deep breath. There was so much she'd like to say to him right now. So, so much. "Yeah."

"I can have the plane there by one. Will that be enough time for you, or is there stuff at the office you need to do?"

"There's stuff I need to do." She had at least four meetings today, and the inspections over every department. She'd moved everything to Thursday when her mom wanted to go to Vegas.

"Oh, so more like this evening?"

"If you're lucky." *Stop. Being angry right now wouldn't solve anything.* "Yeah, this evening is fine. Maybe around seven."

"Are—are you all right?"

"Yep." Just dandy.

"Er, well, I really owe you one. So sorry to throw this on you at the last minute. After we hang up, I'll give Charles a call so he knows to take over. I'll make sure you've got a room out here—and you're welcome to bring someone along, if you'd like. That way, you're not feeling like this is all about work, or whatever. Maybe get a free vacation out of it."

Why did he have to bring up Charles? He had no idea how lame he sounded. But she also knew her mom would *never* forgive her if she found out she'd gone to Vegas anyway. "Actually, I was planning on coming down with someone this weekend. Would it be okay to bring them a bit early?"

"Wow." He attempted a nervous chuckle. "So, that explains why you told me no. You've already got plans to elope."

She rolled her eyes. "Yes, yes I do."

CHAPTER TWELVE:

Will started to cough. Hard. Good. Maybe he'd choke to death.

"You okay?" Eliza grinned as she switched the cell to her other ear.

"Yeah." He hacked a bit more. "Sorry. Just surprised, I guess."

"Serves you right."

"So, uh, what's his name?" His voice sounded a bit more gravelly.

Why is he such a dork? "There is no guy, Will. I was being sarcastic."

"Oh." He paused a second. "But you *are* bringing someone with you?"

"Yes."

"Someone you've planned on traveling to Las Vegas with for a while now?"

"Yes."

"Oh, okay. So, it's a friend or something?"

She laughed. "You're as bad as my mother."

She could almost imagine his answering grin. "Sorry. Just curious, I guess."

"Hmm… I know that feeling well. Especially over an email I can't read."

He sounded worried. "Did you read it?"

"No. I told you I wouldn't, so I haven't." Good grief.

"Oh, I wondered if that's why you're mad at me."

Oh, no—it was way worse than any letter. "Even when I try to hide it, it still shows, huh?"

"Eliza, I've known you long enough to guess if you're ticked off at me again or not. I mean, how much of our partnership has been upsetting to you?"

Was she always angry? She was, wasn't she? She couldn't wait to find fault with him. "Well, when you put it that way . . ."

"So, to answer your question, yes, it shows. I guess I just know you too well." He hesitated and then asked, "Would you like to talk about it?"

"Now? Oh, heck, no. Your sister is first. And then we'll discuss my issues."

"Do you want to know one of my pet peeves?"

The kettle whistled. "Sure," she said as she poured hot water into the mug.

"It drives me nuts to have unresolved issues."

"Oh, I know that." She put the kettle back on the stove and turned off the burner. "I'm the exact same way. You have no idea how badly I'd like to discuss this with you."

"In other words, you mean, tell me off?" His voice began to sound tired and groggy again.

She almost felt sorry for him. Almost. "Yep. And it's a doozey."

"Nice." He sighed. "Is there any way I can apologize for it now, tell you I'm an idiot, and we chalk it up to growth and change and...?"

Her heart softened, just slightly. "Don't." She took a deep breath. "Look, here's the thing. I promise to be calm and as rational as possible when we can talk about this face-to-face."

"Thank you." He groaned, and then his voice changed. "Oh, Eliza, I'm just screwing everything up, aren't I? I feel like I've messed up so much that I'm finally face-to-face with karma."

"Hey," she said. "It's okay. We're all stupid—we all do dumb things. It's how we handle them afterward that matters."

"I don't know. I see my little sister asleep in the other room, knowing Joe has literally devastated her. I can't . . . I can't even function when I think of how much I'd like to repay him for his actions to her, right now. I have no words for the amount of fury…"

"Okay, Will. It's okay. I'm coming. I'll be there as soon as I can. Maybe I can swap some of these appointments to next week."

His voice cracked. "Why? Why would you be so willing to help me?"

"I don't know—I just know I feel this pull to be there right now." She looked blindly toward the sink, not willing to address the emotions swirling through her. "I'm so sorry to cause more drama this morning. I . . . seriously, my stuff can wait. Don't think about it. It's just a misunderstanding anyway, I'm sure. Right now, let's help get some of this weight off your shoulders. It's too much for anyone to bear alone."

He inhaled a ragged breath.

"Can you talk about what Georgia went through at all?" She bit her lip, not knowing how to ask what she'd like to know without overstepping boundaries.

"Oh, it was bad, Eliza, it was so, so bad. And she's only shared a portion of it. This is going to be a long healing process for her. She was in love with him. She thought they'd live happily ever after…" Will grumbled a few words and then whispered tersely, "And what she got was beaten, sexually assaulted, and left with nothing except the reality that this world was too cruel—too real—too painful to live in."

Eliza gasped. The horror of his words chilled her instantly. The poor, poor girl. "Send the plane at one. I'll be there. And email me your address and the list as soon as possible. I'm sorry, Will—I'm so sorry." She couldn't even begin to imagine what she'd do if such a thing had happened to her sister. She closed her eyes. It was better to remain calm and not hit something. "We'll figure this out. We're going to make this better for her. I promise."

"I'm so lost, I'll take any help I can get. Thank you."

As soon as Eliza hung up with Will, she called her mother. It would seem that seven a.m. was early for her too. "Elizabeth?"

"Mom, how soon can you be ready to head to Vegas?"

"What? Are you kidding?" She could hear her mom rustling around with the covers of her bed.

"Yes. I know, sorry. Change of plans."

"Eliza, I swear you'll be the death of me. How soon are you planning on leaving? You don't mean today, do you?"

"Yes, today. This afternoon."

"Ack! I can't go this afternoon. I have a lot of stuff to do before we leave!"

"Will Darcy's private jet will be here at one to pick us up."

Her mother gasped. "Well, why didn't you say so? I'll be ready in ten minutes."

CHAPTER THIRTEEN:

After a frantic morning of phone calls and moving meetings and dealing with worried team leaders, Eliza was finally able to calm down enough to breathe. She didn't even go into the office that morning and chose to relay all information from home. While on the phone, she'd been packing, and in between calls, she was making to-do lists to guarantee she wouldn't forget anything. Then, of course, once that was all done came the tidying up and making sure the house didn't have smelly trash left in it the whole weekend.

About three hours later, she was finally opening up the email about Georgia's things. She printed off the list and directions to Will's house. Eliza was surprised to find out that he lived right there in Bountiful, not too far from her. How was it that she'd never actually seen his house before? There had been plenty of invitations, all mostly business parties and the like, but it'd seem she'd managed to shy away from every single one.

She typed the address to the home on Hidden Ridge Circle into her phone and tucked Georgia's list into her purse. Then she followed the directions from the email to the bank on Main Street. After speaking with the teller—

who Will called earlier—and showing her I.D., she was given a small manila envelope that contained his extra keys.

It took a bit longer than she thought it would to drive up the mountain to his house. Finally, she punched in the key code at the gate and went up the circular driveway, and then slammed on her brakes. Not that she was traveling fast, but—

There honestly were no words for the gorgeous building before her. None. It was the most stunning revival of a Georgian mansion she'd ever seen. In fact, with the color of the brick, multiple stories, and sprawling wings, it felt as though she had traveled to England.

Her heart caught in her throat, and her hands begin to shake. All at once, she felt incredibly overwhelmed and confused—almost as if this was some practical joke and everyone was in on it but her.

As soon as her fingers stopped shaking enough to dial, she called Will.

"Hello?"

She burst out, "What is this? Where am I?"

He seemed concerned. "What's going on? Are you okay? Are you lost?"

She clutched the keys and slowly got out of her car. "I—I don't know. I think so. I hope so. I swear, if this is some sort of joke, it's not funny, Will."

"Where are you?"

Turning around, she gasped when she saw the amazing views of the city nestled in the valley below her, and the shimmering lake beyond them. It was one of the most breathtaking sights she'd ever seen. "I don't know. I followed the address you gave me, and now I'm at the top of a mountain at this seriously massive mansion, and I…"

He chuckled. "Yeah, it's probably a bit much, isn't it?"

"Shut it. This is yours? Like, really *yours*?"

"I wanted something that would last forever. I studied designs for two years and finally decided on that one. With the help of an incredible architect, we created this crazy big dream home."

"Will?"

"Yeah?"

"I just . . . I don't know—it's . . ."

"You hate it, don't you?"

"What? No! Definitely not. It's overwhelming, but so, so beautiful. I would've never taken you for the Georgian architecture type. The brick, the grand entrance columns, the sculptured window casings—it's like a home straight from when I visited Britain."

"Well, that's what I was going for. Something old worldly that I could transport here."

She shook her head as her eyes roved over the incredible details all around her. "It's like something from a fairy tale."

"Go look inside. You haven't seen anything yet. And tell me what you think of the kitchen. I know you and your kitchens."

Her heart skipped a beat. She knew he didn't mean to make it sound like he wanted her approval of *his* kitchen, but it certainly came off that way. And not that he'd ever need it. It wasn't like she'd ever be living here.

As she walked up to the main doors, Will chatted on about the construction and brick and energy-efficient design—all the technical stuff that went into making the house. She let him talk. Her mind was racing so much over the complexity of such a place that she was only half paying attention anyway. The lock clicked open, and she pushed the French door in.

Stepping into the mansion was unlike anything she'd ever experienced before. A gorgeous sweeping staircase beckoned her onto the gleaming light-colored marble floor. His taste was exquisite, like something you'd see in a magazine or TV show, not in real life. "Oh, wow!" she whispered as she closed the door and walked across the entryway.

"Did you make it in?"

"Just now. It's so pretty, Will. Honestly, amazing."

He seemed excited. "Okay, head to your right. Through the archway, you'll see a hall. Do you see it?"

"Yes."

"Follow it until it ends."

She did, but not before marveling at the artwork, furniture, and tapestries in the rooms she passed by. One looked like a music room, another an elaborate office, and another an ornate dining room, with a long table that could seat at least twenty people. As she got to the end of the hall, she walked through the only archway there—on her left—and then nearly dropped the phone.

It was by far the most stunning gourmet kitchen she'd ever seen. "Look at that stove!" she cried as she practically flew to the large eight-burner glory, her hand gripping the phone. "I would kill to have this stove!"

"Perfect for entertaining, isn't it?" he asked.

"I think if I had something this fun, I'd never make it in to work."

He laughed. "Yeah, it can be hard sometimes."

Everything was spotless. The marble countertops, the shining floors, the sinks—everything. "I'm impressed with how clean the place is. Looks like you've never used it."

"Oh, I use it all right. I just have a maid who comes in and helps a few times a week."

Of course he did. Eliza continued to snoop and pry into as many rooms as she could while Will took her on a sort of virtual phone tour. By the time she'd made it to

Georgia's room, she was almost running late. She still had to pick up her mom and then head over to the airport.

With his help, she was able to collect the things on the list, which included an old iPhone, iPod, some clothes she'd left behind. Then Eliza added some toiletries, cosmetics, and a curling iron, from the vanity in the large ensuite bathroom. She found her robe, blanket, and then about five pairs of shoes. It wasn't on the list, but when Eliza stumbled upon a stash of European chocolates in a nightstand while searching for the old phone, she also grabbed a few of them. She then put everything in a couple of large designer beach bags she'd found in one of the closets, as well as a swimsuit she'd found near the bags.

"There. I think that's everything."

"Actually, could you grab one thing for me?" Will asked.

"Sure. What do you need?"

"My Kindle. I forgot it."

She chuckled. "I should make you read the books on mine—then you'll know what true torture is."

"I take it you're not into mysteries?"

"Nope. Lots of self-help and romance."

He groaned. "You're right. It would be torture."

"So, where to?" She was standing in the middle of the hall with shut doors all around her.

He directed her to his room, and as she opened the door, she halted. There on a small table near his bed was a collection of greeting cards—very familiar cards. She approached and found they were the cards she had given him throughout the year with expressions of congratulations, thanks, or for the different holidays. Nothing much—just appreciation, really. It was bizarre that he'd kept them, and strangely endearing too.

"You're awfully quiet. Did I lose you?" he asked.

Guiltily, she started, and then cleared her throat. "Sorry. Where is it?"

He must've realized what had happened. "Oh, um, stay away from the side tables next to the bed. It'll be by the overstuffed chair near the floor-to-ceiling window, the one facing the fireplace."

She decided not to tease him about the cards just yet—there'd be plenty of time to ask about them later. Instead, she walked over to the Kindle, which was still on its charger, unplugged it, and slipped it into one of his sister's bags. "Okay. That's everything. Can you think of anything else you need?"

"Nope. Just you."

CHAPTER FOURTEEN:

Eliza gave a friendly honk as she pulled up to her parents' house and then got out. As she crossed the threshold, she saw her dad sitting on her mom's luggage watching TV. The suitcases were standing up, smooshed together with his bum rested on top, like they were his own personal stool. "What are you doing?"

He winked and told her to hush.

"Are you going to tease Mom forever?" she asked as she sat down in the comfy chair next to him.

"Well, she's the one who put these here hours ago. I figure they're our furniture now."

She laughed.

Chuckling, he grabbed the remote from a nearby table and turned down the volume. "So, missy, you sure you're up for this trip?"

"With Mom?" She rolled her eyes and sighed. "No. I imagine it'll be the same as it always is."

He nodded. "She's pretty excited about this Darcy fellow."

"I know. She constantly will be."

"So, what do you think about him? Still hate his guts and want to hogtie the varmint?"

"Dad! I never said that."

"Nope." His eyes twinkled. "But you sure thought it a ton, though."

"You know me so well." Her eyebrows rose. "I'm still thinking it now, about every other day."

"Ah, I see. He's starting to wear you down." He wiggled around on the top of the luggage and found a more comfortable spot. "Good. It's about time. That boy's as sweet on you as strawberry jam on ice cream."

"He is?" She leaned back to get a better look at him. "And how would you know?"

"Because your mom's nearly driven me to drinking, and you know I've never had a drink in my life, but that doesn't mean I sure as heck didn't contemplate it at least twice a day for the two years before we got married. And then about four times a day since!"

She grinned, but was a bit lost.

"I knew. I knew the second that I met that gorgeous woman, my life had been completely knocked upside down. I knew I'd never get a day's rest, she was so darn active and constantly worried about all the silliness around her. I knew exactly what my life would be like." He looked up toward the stairs. "But man, I couldn't imagine a day without her brightness, and her downright nosy biddy neighbor attitude. She has kept me level-headed and chuckling every day since."

He glanced over at Eliza, his faded blue eyes searching her wearily. "And she needed me. I'd never felt more loved or needed in my whole life until I met that darned crazy woman. Never. And I knew I'd never find another like her."

Warmth spread through Eliza from head to toe. "I want that, Daddy. I want a man to love me just for being me."

"You're ornerier than a nest of hornets."

"I know." She smiled ruefully.

He waggled his brows. "You're frank, you're exact, and you're tough."

"Gee, Dad, nothing like making me feel good."

"Well, that's another of your faults—you interrupt before a person's finished. Listen, little one. Let people talk—you'll find out a lot more good if you did."

He was right. She was always barging in. This time, she waited.

"You're also caring, kind, thoughtful, and the most giving woman I know." His eyes twinkled. "You're better than any man I know. And only a fool wouldn't fall for you. I tell you now, William Darcy didn't get to be where he is because he's a fool. Nope. He isn't. And he loves you."

A strange sort of calmness came over her. "Why?"

He patted his knees. "Well that's the part you need to listen for and find out yourself. Though, may I suggest you do that when your mom's not around?"

Eliza winced. "Oh, this is going to be so bad."

"Ha!" He shrugged. "It'll be good for the boy to meet his biggest fan."

She'd never heard Will called a boy before. It made her grin. "I guess if he can survive Mom, he can survive anything."

He hollered up the stairs. "Melissa, Eliza's here! Were you gonna come down, or were you planning on sleeping all day?"

"What?" her mom answered. "How long's she been here? Why doesn't anyone tell me anything anymore?" Eliza could hear her moving around above their heads and then walking down the stairs.

"Hi, Mom."

"Let's get going." Melissa brushed at her hair with her fingers. "I've just had a bit of a beauty rest. Now it's time to party."

"Are you sure you wouldn't rather stay here and celebrate with Dad?"

"Ha! And miss out on the chance of seeing my daughter elope? Heck, no."

"Hey, now. What's this about eloping?" Her dad winked at her. "I didn't survive cancer just to find out about some wedding later. I'd better be walking you down the aisle, or you'd better believe your young man won't have legs to walk around with!"

Eliza shook her head. "I'm not eloping with anyone. You two are certifiably crazy, you know that?" She stood up and gave her dad a hug.

"Yep." He chuckled. "And remember, you're part of our gene pool. You don't stand a chance."

"Besides, Dad and Jane have a weekend of chess planned without us." Mom said as she walked over to the door and scooped her purse off the floor.

"Yep." Dad patted his stomach. "Pizza, movies, chess, and Oreo ice cream."

Mom wagged her finger. "You promised you wouldn't eat too much junk food."

He laughed. "I promise only to eat enough to truly celebrate your birthday without me."

Suddenly, her mom gasped. "Michael Martin Bennet! Get off my luggage now! What in the world do you think you're doing, sitting on it like it's living room furniture?"

"Well, isn't it?"

"Oomph." She pushed against him. "I can't believe this. It's like you're still a ten-year-old boy sometimes."

He nearly split a gut laughing at her outraged face as he stood up.

Eliza just shook her head and began hauling the nearest suitcase out to her car. "One of these days, I'm sure I'll need therapy."

"Ain't good enough upbringing if you don't!" her dad hollered after her as he brought the other suitcase with him. He gently nudged her away and loaded them both into the trunk. Then he shut it and said seriously, "Take good care of her."

"I will."

He nodded and gave her a big hug. "Love you. Be safe." Then he turned, caught his wife up, and dipped her in a movie-style kiss. One foot popped up above them both.

"Michael!" she gasped and giggled as he kept kissing her.

"What? I have to get as much as I can now to make up for all the days I can't while you're gone."

Eliza got in the car and chuckled. No one could ever say that those two didn't deserve each other. And thank goodness for that.

CHAPTER FIFTEEN:

Eliza's mom chattered happily the whole way to the local airport, and while they were ushered onto the tarmac—via Will's instructions—and onto the awaiting plane. The pilot met them at the door, introducing himself and the other crew member on board, a flight attendant who was also a certified pilot in case of an emergency.

Both men were cordial and professional and quick, and soon they were zooming thousands of feet in the air. The whole flight wasn't expected to take more than an hour or so. After snacks had been served, and her mom satisfied, the attendant left them alone.

"Wow. This is one of the coolest things I've ever done!" Mom gushed.

"Me too," Eliza said with a small grin on her face.

"So now that we're alone, tell me what happened. I thought we weren't going because you were mad at Mr. Darcy, and then the next thing I know, we *are* going, and he's sending his jet to get us. Now, where's the rest of the story?"

Eliza chewed her lip. She wasn't sure how much she could or should actually say. It technically wasn't her story to tell. "An emergency came up, and Will asked me to bring some stuff for him. Then, because it was so last minute and he felt bad for disrupting my plans, he offered to fly out anyone else I'd like to bring with me." She put her chair into a full reclining position. "I knew that if you found out I went to Vegas without you, you'd kill me. So, here we are. It's just that simple."

"No, it isn't." Mom gave a smug smile and reclined her chair as well. "I'm not saying that what you're saying isn't true—it just isn't the whole truth. But don't worry, I'll get it out of you eventually. I always do."

Actually, she didn't. But she didn't need to know that.

"These leather seats are so comfortable. I never knew it could be this wonderful to fly somewhere. Now I'm going to be spoiled rotten," her mom said.

"I know what you mean. I'm almost there myself."

Her mom sat up. "That settles it. You have to marry Will Darcy just so I can fly in the lap of luxury."

She rolled her eyes. "Yeah, Mom, that's the *exact* reason why I'd marry Will."

Her mom popped some chocolate-covered almonds in her mouth. "See? I'm wearing you down already. You didn't say you *wouldn't* marry him this time."

"Only because I know it'd be useless." Eliza closed her eyes. It was the first real moment she'd had to relax since waking up that morning.

"Do you know what I think?"

"Hmm?"

"I think you should give him a chance."

"And why's that? Because he's rich?" Eliza chuckled. "Do you have any idea how shallow that sounds?"

Her mom giggled. "Yes." Then she sighed. "No, I really don't care deep down how wealthy he is, though it is an amazing perk—don't get me wrong! I just want you settled down with someone who makes you feel alive."

"And you think Will Darcy makes me feel alive? Ha! I feel more like killing someone." Eliza looked over, caught her mom's happy grin, and then closed her eyes again.

"No, dear, I have hope for him because as soon as you started working for Mr. Darcy, you woke up."

She scrunched her brow. "What do you mean?"

"I mean, something sparked inside you—something felt more real. For the first time, you allowed someone to get under your skin and annoy you. You *felt* things."

"I felt a headache coming on," Eliza groaned through a grin. "Kind of like now."

"Say what you want, but sooner or later, you'll realize I'm right."

"Okay, Mom. Can we please behave? Just try not to embarrass me in front of my boss. Please?" She smirked. It was hopeless.

"You're no fun."

"Ha! Excuse me for avoiding awkward situations. I kind of make it a rule not to openly humiliate myself if I can." What was it about moms and their love of embarrassing their daughters?

"Is he okay?"

Eliza opened her eyes and looked over at her mom. "Who? Will?"

"Yes. I'm worried about why you had to rush to Vegas. Is he okay?"

"You know, Mom, it amazes me you can change subjects so quickly."

"Is that a yes or a no?"

Eliza took a deep breath. "No. He's not okay."

"Ah. Anything I can do to help?"

"I don't know. But let's keep things low key, please. The less stress he has to deal with, the better."

"Is this business stress?"

"Good grief. You're relentless." Eliza chuckled to take the sting out of her words. "And no, it's not business. This is all personal." She turned toward her mom. "And it has *nothing* to do with me."

Her mom's gaze met hers. She searched Eliza's eyes for a few moments before pulling away and nodding. "Okay. You win. I'll behave myself. Though you won't tell me anything, really, and will completely keep me in the dark, I'll behave."

"Still not getting it out of me, Mom. This isn't mine to tell."

"Well, can't blame me for trying."

Eliza shook her head and turned back around, snuggling into the seat. "However, I believe this trip might be a good thing after all."

"And why's that?"

"Because maybe after being around Will for so long, you'll finally feel like strangling him too. Then I won't have to hear all this nonsense about marriage all the time."

"Elopement, dear. We've upgraded now that we're in Vegas, remember?"

"Huh." She closed her eyes again and thought about her dad's threat. "I take that back. A part of me really has to wonder what he'd look like without legs."

CHAPTER SIXTEEN:

Will was there as they stepped off the plane, and Eliza's heart betrayed her by doing the oddest little somersault right in the airport. He was all smiles as he approached and surprised her by collecting her up in a huge hug, his long arms going all the way around her and tucking her in close. Eliza's hands were each carrying one of Georgia's bags, so she held her arms out wide.

"I'm so glad you're here," he whispered in her ear before releasing her.

"I can see that." Flustered, she turned and gestured toward her mom, whose jaw was nearly on the floor. "This is my mom, Melissa Bennet."

"So you're the friend she's chosen to bring." He gave Eliza a short look as he collected Georgia's things. "Let me help you with your bags too, Mrs. Bennet."

"Thank you, Mr. Darcy," her mom gushed. "Your plane was so comfortable."

The flight attendant brought up the rear with Eliza's suitcase.

"I'm glad you enjoyed yourself," Will said to her mom. "But please feel free to call me Will."

"Of course. And use Melissa for me. Mrs. Bennet was my mother-in-law."

Will laughed and then turned to the attendant. "Jeff, could you take that to the car for us? Thanks."

Eliza figured it was time to explain. "It's my mom's birthday this weekend, so we were coming to celebrate."

"Ah, I see." Will grinned over at her. "I take it you're turning thirty-five?"

She laughed. "Of course!"

"I thought so." He turned and winked at Eliza and then asked quietly, "How are you? Did you survive the trip?"

Her gaze met his, and she nodded. "I'm going to assume that *my* past hour has been much more enjoyable than yours. How's she doing?"

He glanced over at her mom. "How much have you said to her?" he whispered.

"Nothing."

Will nodded. "Thank you. Let's talk when we get Melissa settled in. And then I'll introduce you to Georgia tonight—that is, if you'd like to meet her."

"I'd love that more than anything."

Will paused at the door and let her mother walk past. Then, as Eliza followed, he said, "Good. She's really excited to meet you."

"Me?" Eliza looked back as she stepped through the door, and Will allowed it to shut behind him. "Why me?"

As he glanced around the noisy airport, she could've sworn he looked flustered. "Why not?" He then focused the rest of his conversation on her mom. "So, what would you like to do while you're here? You're the birthday girl. You get to pick."

Eliza blocked out her mom's happy chatter as they approached the car. Melissa was in her element, talking to the one person she'd hoped to talk to most. It was time Eliza backed off and allowed those two to finally meet.

"Eliza, would you like to sit in back with Will?" her mom asked.

She looked up. "No, I'm a little tired. You two gab. I'll ride in front with the driver."

Will gave her a funny look.

And she grinned. It'd be good for him.

When he turned to her mom, he was all smiles. "That's right. I'd rather talk to you anyway. I already see Eliza at work all day. So, tell me more about what you'd like to do."

The hotel was stunning, and Will had clearly spared no expense. Eliza and her mom were set up in a gorgeous two-bedroom suite. It even had its own kitchen, dining room, living room, and balcony.

"This is unbelievable!" her mom gasped as she wandered from room to room.

Even Eliza was a bit taken aback. "Will, this *is* ridiculous. We only needed a small hotel room."

He shook his head. "It was nothing, believe me. A gift from the owner." He wheeled her mom's luggage into the living room. "Which bedroom do you claim, Melissa?"

"The blue one! I love the contrast with all the brown floral arrangements. It's so pretty."

"Very well, the blue and brown one it is." He followed her mom into the room.

Eliza wandered into the other bedroom and found very elegant gray and yellow décor. The bed looked sumptuous with all its accent pillows. There was a small bowl of fruit and snacks on the nightstand, and bottles of water nearly everywhere.

"Do you like it?" Will asked from her doorway.

She spun around and shook her head in amazement. "I can't imagine how much this cost."

"Then stop worrying about it. Besides, I know the owner—he's returning a favor. Oh, and there's no charge for anything you eat or drink. It's all part of the ticket, including room service." He reached into his pocket, pulled out an envelope, and handed it to Eliza. "There's a bunch of five-dollar bills in there. Use them for tips."

"Wow. You've thought of everything, haven't you? But really, you don't need to."

"One less thing you have to worry about."

She opened the envelope and gasped. There had to be fifty bills. "This is way too much."

He waved her off. "It's no big deal. If you don't use them all, you can give them back. But for now, don't worry about it."

"I can't even imagine using them all."

"They go fast, trust me. Let me know if you run out, and I'll be sure to bring some more down." He pointed toward the ceiling. "Georgia and I are in the room above yours at the top, so if you need anything, don't hesitate to call, and I'll be here. Or just show up yourself, if you want."

"So this is where you went off to." Her mom came in the room and smiled.

"Are you hungry? What are you thinking for dinner?" Will asked her mom.

She looked back and forth between the two of them and then said, "Did I overhear you correctly? Is room service free?"

"Yes."

She suddenly let out a big fake yawn and raised a hand to her forehead. "Goodness. I'm a bit wiped out from all the traveling." She patted her mouth for emphasis. "I think I'd rather take advantage of that jetted tub in my bathroom and order some room service tonight. And probably hit the hay early."

Good grief. "Mom, you don't have to stay in." Eliza wasn't buying her act one bit.

"Yes, I do. I'm super tired. Don't worry about me, though. Go out and have some fun." She waved her hand at the two of them. "I mean it. You both shoo! I'd really like the place to myself."

Yeah, this wasn't awkward at all. What if Will didn't want to hang out with her so long? "I don't have a problem staying in. I've got some emails to catch up on anyway, if you'd rather have an easy night." She glanced over at Will, giving him a way out if he needed one.

"You work every day. Take the time off. Besides, it's your mom's birthday weekend. You have to do what she says."

"Yeah, he's right." Her mom grinned.

Eliza's eyebrow rose as she placed one hand on her hip. "Oh, really?"

Will looped his arm through Eliza's and pulled her next to him. "Don't worry about a thing, Melissa. We'll have fun tonight, and I'll bring her back in time to get enough sleep to party all day tomorrow."

"Perfect." Her mom actually clapped—the traitor.

Will began to tug on Eliza's arm as if to take her out the door right then. "Wait, wait. I'm not leaving this hotel room until I've changed. So forget it." She glanced at the clock. "It's three p.m. now, so—"

"You've got until six, and then I'll come get you," he said as he headed toward the door. "And Melissa, please let me know if you need anything at all."

Her mom waved. "I will. Thank you, dear."

He gave Eliza one final look. "Bye, you two. Eliza, six sharp. Be ready."

CHAPTER SEVENTEEN:

When Will approached the door of Eliza's suite at six o'clock sharp, he was a nervous wreck. He'd been standing in the hallway for over ten minutes already, since he was a nerd and couldn't wait another moment and came too early. Of course, it didn't help that his sister was making him edgy. When he'd told Georgia that Eliza was here, she began to perk up immediately, but when he asked if she'd like to join them for dinner, that darn girl insisted on staying in the hotel room. However, she was so excited to meet her later that night, she ended up changing her outfit three times before he left. Of course, it helped that she finally had some clothes again.

This was it. The breaking point for him. He didn't understand the building pressure, but he knew something major was about to happen. If anyone could help Georgia get over this awful bump, it would be Eliza. She was the best at fixing any situation—how could she not excel at emotional fixes too?

He wiped his hands on his new jeans and took a deep breath. There was too much riding on this, on Eliza's willingness to help. What if she failed him? What if she didn't want to get involved in the drama of an emotionally lost teenager? What if she hated teens? Or what if she was everything he had ever imagined and more, and what if he fell even more in love with her than he already had? Has. Had. Whatever.

The point was—then what? These next couple of days were no longer about desperation—they were literally about his breaking point. How much longer could he last, pretending they were just friends? How much further could his heart stretch before it snapped?

And the worst was—could he handle the rejection a second time? Ugh. Okay. He was way overthinking everything. It must be what a woman feels like, having her brain constantly worrying over things that haven't even happened. He took a deep breath and knocked on the door.

There. Breathe. Stay cool. Stay calm. And instead of driving yourself crazy with worry, you should be enjoying this moment right now. And nothing else.

When Eliza opened the door, he inhaled so sharply, he started coughing right in the hallway. Like an absolute moron.

"Are you okay?"

"Yeah," he sputtered out as he finally got control of his breathing again. "You look really nice, by the way." He was pretty sure this was the first time he'd ever seen her in a dress. Her hair was curled too. It was different. Softer, more feminine. He liked it.

She looked down. "Thanks. I hope it isn't too dressy. It was a gift. Casinos aren't my thing, so I wasn't really sure what to wear." Her eyes followed his more casual jeans and buttoned-up shirt.

"No. It's fine." He had no idea what other women wore to casinos either, and he was pretty sure he'd still have no idea what they wore by the end of tonight. There was no one else he'd be watching. "Are you ready to go?"

"My mom's taking a bubble bath, so we can go whenever. I don't need to say good-bye."

Eliza was clearly rambling. They probably both sounded like teenagers heading out on their first date. He noticed that her hands shook a bit as she clutched her small purse. She was as nervous as he was. Good. "I thought we might get a bite to eat and then head up to my suite and meet Georgia."

Her huge smile lit up the whole hallway. "I'd love that. I'm really excited to meet her."

He couldn't believe how easily she caused his heart to skip a beat. "She's got a surprise for you when we come home. I mean, back. When we come back from dinner." He cleared his throat and looked away. Right.

Eliza giggled and then closed the door behind her. "It sounds wonderful. I love surprises."

"You do?" He glanced over at the beautiful woman next to him as they began to head down the hall. How he'd love to surprise her daily.

"Yep." She took a deep breath. "So, where would you like to go? What are you in the mood for?"

"Well, since you're my date, I thought you should pick."

She paused. "Is . . . is this a date, then?"

Their eyes met. "I—" *Yes. No. Wasn't it? This is why women are so dang confusing. You have no idea what they're really thinking. Ever.* She looked scared. "Not if you don't want it to be. We can just hang out as friends. That's cool too."

He could see myriad emotions flinging themselves around in that head of hers. She was just as much out of her depth as he was. Will decided to put her out of her misery. "You know what, don't worry about it. No, it's not a date. But I'm paying, as a thank you for helping me out. How does that sound?"

She stepped forward in the hallway, still staring right at him.

"Okay?" He was so close, they could almost touch. And yet, she still didn't say a word to him. If he'd ever wished he had a superhero power, reading minds would be the top of his list. Then again, if he could read her mind, none of this ridiculous angst would exist. This pull of not knowing, of wishing, hoping—yet so uncertain. There was definitely something to be said about the unknown that was completely thrilling.

"You're arrogant, and you destroy love," she suddenly blurted out. "You hurt people I care about. And you're the last man I could ever imagine myself dating." Then she shocked him by grabbing his shirt, pulling his head down, and kissing him.

Wow, did she kiss him! And kiss him. *Is this actually happening? Um—women really needed to come with instruction manuals. Seriously.*

After the initial shock wore off, he happily wrapped his arms around her and began to return the kiss, never wanting to release his mouth from those sweet lips again. Heck, if she was all for it, who was he to argue? *Wow.*

When she finally pulled away—because there was no way on earth it was going to be him—she panted and glared at him. "And don't ever expect something like that from me again."

Things just got a whole lot more interesting. He didn't know where the unexpected confidence came from, but boy, it was refreshing. He grinned. "This is definitely a date." Elizabeth Bennet may hate his living guts, but she loved him. He knew that much, even if *she* didn't.

"It isn't."

"Oh, it is." He began to walk forward. "You've taken away every bit of doubt in my mind. And you'd better believe I'm going to enjoy each second of it." He held out a hand, which surprisingly, she took, easily slipping her much smaller fingers into his. "Now, you'd better hurry up and choose what's for dinner, or I'll pick—and I'll choose you. Those lips of yours are much too tempting not to try again."

"You're impossible." Clearly flustered, she looked away, but he could see her stifling a grin.

He nudged her shoulder with his. "You know you loved it."

She rolled her eyes and picked up the pace. "Just as much as I love spiders."

CHAPTER EIGHTEEN

Eliza was in way over her head. She knew it as soon as Will mentioned they were on a date. Did he still like her? Was he trying to string her along so he could dump her later? Get her back for rejecting him? And then to kiss him! What in the world was she thinking? He'd been smiling at her ever since. It was strange and different and completely terrifying to find herself wanting to see where this went, to see how long they could actually get along.

She'd decided on seafood, and he took her to a pretty posh restaurant. She could tell they had their freshly caught fish imported every day. And the atmosphere, while casual, had a certain flair and opulence to it.

The waiter took them to a secluded booth and then placed a menu on the table that displayed no prices, which, from her experience, meant this place was very, very expensive. One day, she'd have to take Will out for a hot dog and hamburger just to see what he'd do with normal food.

"You certainly repay favors well," she said as she nodded toward the menu.

He looked a bit worried. "It is too much? Would you rather go to someplace like Red Lobster or something?"

"It *is* too much." She shrugged. "But I'm okay. We can definitely eat here, as long as I never know how much it actually cost."

He grinned. "Deal."

When another waiter came up with wine, Will looked over at Eliza first. When she shook her head, he declined for them both. Instead, she sipped on her imported water.

They ordered their meal, and then the awkwardness began to sink in. It was only them, all alone, staring at each other.

He started with the same things he asked earlier. "How was the flight? Do you like your room? Was it difficult to get the meetings swapped to Monday?"

She answered them again, giving the same replies as before, and then allowed her voice to trail off.

Yes, it was fun to kiss Will and get caught up in the drama and romanticism of a large house and fancy airplane, but the reality was, they really didn't know each other. They simply had nothing to talk about.

Will must've been thinking the exact same thing, because he suddenly leaned forward. "Tell me about yourself."

She sat up a little straighter. At least this was a start. "Well, what would you like to know?"

He shrugged. "I'm not sure. Anything, really. What's your favorite pet? Was there an animal you loved more than the rest when you were younger?"

She grinned and glanced down at the untouched china and silverware at the table. "You won't believe it." She picked up a salad fork and began to draw lazy circles on the linen tablecloth with it.

"A skunk is about the only thing I wouldn't believe you'd like."

"A skunk!" She chuckled and then scrunched her brow. "They're actually kind of cute, but no. My pet was a unicorn."

Now it was his turn to look surprised. His eyebrows rose, and he failed miserably at trying to wipe the smile off his face. "A unicorn? *That* was your favorite pet? Not a kitten or dog?

"Oh, I liked those too. Just not as much." She lifted her nose at him. "No young lady of consequence would be without her pet unicorn, of course."

He cleared his throat and asked as seriously as he could, "So you actually had one?"

"Of course! We almost had two, but then Jane changed her mind at the last minute and decided she wanted a dragon instead."

He chuckled. "And what did you name your unicorn?"

"Mr. Sparkles," she said with an absolutely straight face.

"Indeed. And what did your sister name her dragon?"

Eliza dropped the fork. As soon as Will mentioned Jane, the mood fell flat. It made no sense, since she was the one to bring her up, but all at once, she was tired of playing. She tried to brush the feeling aside, but found that she couldn't. "I don't remember." She sighed agitatedly and stood up. "Excuse me. I'm going to find the restroom."

She felt a moment of guilt at his stricken face as she walked away, but quickly shoved the feeling aside. Jane deserved so much better than this. Eliza followed the signs to the nearest bathroom and walked in.

It was a very fancy room, with velvet couches and bottles of lotions and tissues and everything. Sitting down on the nearest couch, she put her head in her hands and took some deep breaths. He was the enemy. Here she was, flirting with the man who had made it his business to hurt her sister.

Eliza shook her head, attempting to shake out this crazy. What was wrong with her? She seemed to be flip-flopping worse than a freshly caught fish. The analogy suddenly made her stomach churn. Blindly, she looked at the painting on the wall across from where she was sitting. That's exactly what this felt like, being caught on Will Darcy's hook, thrashing back and forth.

She was here for one reason and one reason only—to help her boss with his sister, who'd been through a nightmare and might need a woman to talk to. That was it. Anything else that might develop was as useless and as painful as Will's hook. Yes, he was fun to kiss. Yes, for a moment, she couldn't blame herself for being captured in the surreal romanticism of it all. But when all was said and done, he valued wealth over relationships. He had to, or why else would he think Jane was just after Charles's money? Money would always come first to him.

The hotel, the restaurant, the house. He wouldn't know how to live frugally if he tried. This was how he impressed, how he chose to live. And it wasn't her. It would never be her. And she'd sure as heck better get it through her head now that this life wasn't ever meant to be hers.

By the time Eliza made it back to the table, their dinner was just arriving, almost as if the wait staff had been watching the bathroom door to time it precisely so that their meals were hot and fresh. It was a bit creepy.

However, the food was marvelous. They ate quickly, and Eliza kept the conversation away from anything uncomfortable. At first, Will tried to pry, but after a few failed attempts, he kept the peace and they both stayed on safer, more polite, and less personal subjects. By time the meal was over and they were on their way back to the hotel, Eliza had completely convinced herself that she and Will would only ever be friends—perhaps not even that. Maybe just a little more than acquaintances.

That was, until she met the adorable Georgia Darcy.

CHAPTER NINETEEN:

Georgia beamed when she met them at the door as they walked into Will's suite. "Hello? You must be Eliza," she said as she shook her hand. Eliza could see that her smile didn't quite reach her eyes, and there was still a trace of a bruise on her forehead. "It's nice to meet you." The pretty girl wore one of the maxi dresses Eliza had packed for her. Her hair was twisted into a side braid, and she was adorably barefoot. She led them into a mirror of Eliza's suite. Only the décor was different. Its shades of red and light brown worked well with the darker contrast of the wooden furniture.

Eliza warmed to Georgia instantly. "It's wonderful to finally meet *you*. In all the time I've worked with your brother, I've never met any of his family."

Will shut the door and hugged his sister. "She's practically all the family I've got."

The girl grinned and then pushed her big brother away. "It's not true, and you know it. Don't forget Dad."

Will kicked off his shoes, unbuttoned the top button on his shirt, and then plopped down on the couch. "Well, it's not like he's ever home anyway. He's pretty easy to forget."

Georgia chided him and sat down on the couch with him, curling her feet underneath her long dress, then looked up at Eliza. "Make yourself at home."

Eliza set her purse on the floor next to Will's shoes and occupied the loveseat across from them. It was soft and inviting.

Will grinned. "You can take your shoes off too, if you'd like."

Suddenly, she felt like a fool. "Oh, sorry. You guys are probably one of those polite families who take their shoes off at the door, huh?" She slipped off her heels.

Georgia giggled. It sounded a bit forced. "Of course not. We just don't like shoes. Neither of us."

Eliza's eyebrows rose. "Really? I can't imagine Will not wearing them."

He wiggled his toes in his socks. "Nope. I like my feet free."

It was then that she noticed they were Ghostbuster socks. "They're so cool!"

"Thanks." He smiled over at his sister. "Georgia got them for me."

"Serious? They're really fun."

"Yep." She reached down and grabbed one of his wiggling toes. "He has a whole collection from me."

"It's true. I think I've got the best collection of socks ever."

"I got him Batman, Superman, the Hulk... you name it."

"She even got me an old-school Animaniacs pair."

"No way." Eliza was impressed. "I used to love that show."

He looked over at her. "Me too." Then he ruffled Georgia's hair. "I think I probably have a hundred pairs of socks now, thanks to this one."

"Hey! Watch the hair."

"Yeah, Will," Eliza joined in. "Watch the hair. It's way too pretty to mess up."

Surprisingly, Georgia got up and plopped down next to Eliza. "Yeah, us girls have to stick together." She searched Eliza's gaze as if she were begging for acceptance.

"I see how it is. You're ganging up on me now. Fine." Will rolled over and lay all the way down on the couch, putting his feet up on the armrest. "There. Now I get the whole thing to myself."

Georgia rolled her eyes. "Sorry he's such a dork. Our mom did raise him better than that, I promise."

"I can hear you."

"Good."

"Your mom?" Eliza prodded, curious. "Is she with your dad right now?"

A little bit of a shadow fell over Georgia's face, and Eliza regretted her words instantly. The girl didn't even have to speak—Eliza knew what had happened to her.

"Mom died about ten years ago. From breast cancer."

"Oh, I'm so sorry. Forgive me. I shouldn't have brought her up." Eliza felt awful.

The girl shrugged. "It's okay. It was hard when it happened, and I miss her like crazy sometimes, but it's okay."

"I really didn't mean to go heavy on you the first five minutes of sitting down."

Georgia placed an arm on the back of the loveseat. "You kind of look like her old pictures."

"Me?" Eliza tucked her feet underneath her. "What makes you say that?"

"I don't know—you just do. Look, Will. Doesn't she look like Mom?"

Eliza was afraid to meet his eyes, so she studied the girl while Georgia studied her.

"A little. I never thought about it before."

"Even your hair is the same color."

This was slightly uncomfortable, so she changed the focus away from her. "What was she like?"

Georgia sighed. "Perfect. Soft, kind, caring. Always quiet."

Eliza smiled. Nothing like her, then. They just had similar coloring. "She sounds like an angel."

"She was," Will said. "Unbelievably shy and angelic. Sometimes we wonder how she and Dad ever found each other."

"He's very loud and boisterous and opinionated." Georgia stifled a grin.

Will cleared his throat and sat back up. "That's one way to put it. Dad is well—Dad."

"So, what do you like to do?" the girl asked her.

"Me? I . . . well, I like to watch TV and—"

"Read romance books." Will shuddered.

"Hey! You could learn a lot from a hero of one of those books, you know," Eliza protested.

"Like what?" Will stood up and walked to the adjoining high-backed chair next to her. "Fifty shades of gross?"

Eliza rolled her eyes and turned toward him. "I'll have you know, there happen to be wonderful books out there that deal with the romance aspect of love. They're not always about whatever it is men think women need to be happy. Good grief. I'm talking about real men who love women and will do anything for them to prove it."

He stared at her for a few seconds and then said, "It's books like those that ruin you women for good."

"Of all the sexist things to say!" She was about to stand, but he put his hand up.

"Hear me out for a minute."

Folding her arms, she took a deep breath and sat back in the cushions of the couch. Her father's words about her never listening came back loud and clear. "I'm listening."

"I believe that some—I'm not saying all—but some of those romance books must completely skew the reality of what men really are. You women gush and sigh and long for this impossibly romantic weirdo you've just read about, then toss aside the actual normal man right next to you because he's not Damien, or Alfonzo, or Luke."

"Alfonzo?"

Georgia giggled.

"Whatever. The point is, you say I'm sexist, yet I'm not the one reading about some perfect hero who will guarantee that anyone you meet will never be *man* enough for you."

"You've got to be kidding me." Eliza laughed. "Forgive me for wanting to read about men who don't exist. Fine. I admit it. By your standards, maybe I am sexist. But honestly, have you met the men out there? Why do you think women need to escape so badly?" She leaned forward. "In fact, if I did a study right now on the effects of reading escapist romance, I bet I'd find that it actually *saves* more relationships than it ruins."

"How so?" Now he folded his arms.

"Because despite what you think, women are not stupid creatures who go all gaga over some dream Alfonzo"—she tried not to gag over his name—"and we know for a fact that men aren't like the ones we read about. However, we're able to relate to similar attributes of those heroes, which then allows us to look at our husbands or boyfriends or whatever, and fall in love with them all over again." She flipped her hair over her shoulder. "So really, we're doing you a favor by reading it because it allows us to still want a man when we're done."

"She's got a point, you know." Georgia laughed.

"Oh, no." He pointed at her. "Don't you go starting on me. One woman telling me off is enough for tonight. I definitely don't need two!"

"You know what I've decided, Eliza?" Georgia tapped her shoulder.

Eliza turned toward her. "And what's that?"

"I've decided that Will was right. You are someone I'd love."

Eliza chuckled. "I don't know if 'love' is the right word."

"Anyone who can hold their own against the great Will Darcy deserves respect in my book. And what's not to love about that?"

"Well, when you put it that way, I have no idea."

Both girls laughed.

"Ha. Ha." Will pretended to pout. "I'm feeling completely outnumbered."

"As you should!" Georgia teased. "It's about time you knew how I feel when you and Dad get together."

"Didn't you say you had a surprise for Eliza?" he asked in an obvious attempt to change the subject.

"Oh!" She jumped up. "I nearly forgot. Come on," she said as she ran to the kitchen. "Will told me what your favorite dessert was, so I wanted to make it for you."

Will caught Eliza's arm as she was about to follow. "Thank you," he whispered.

"For?"

"Making her forget. I could never repay you for this. Never."

"Here it is!" Georgia exclaimed. She turned around with a pretty two-layered chocolate frosted cake. "I even did the roses myself."

CHAPTER TWENTY:

"It looks awesome." Eliza walked forward and took the cake from the girl's extended hands. "Thank you so much. I never would've known you made this. I would've thought it came from a bakery." It really was incredible.

"See, Will? Even she thinks so." Georgia pushed past her brother to walk with Eliza to the table.

"You've got some talent," Eliza said.

"Oh, don't say that yet. I can make things beautiful, but how about you taste it before you rave about talent."

"This is true." Will pulled out a dining room chair and sat down. "The real test is trying it. You never know with Georgia."

"Hey. You'd better be nice to me." The girl went to the kitchen. "Eliza, you stay with Will and make sure he doesn't snitch any of the frosting. I'll get the plates."

Eliza pulled out a chair and sat down across from him. "Did you hear that?" She brought the cake closer to her. "I have to watch out and make sure you don't eat any."

"You'd better. I've been known to devour whole cakes in a single sitting."

Eliza shook her head. "I won't even say how disturbing I think that statement is."

He winked. "That's because you clearly don't have brothers. If you had some, you'd know it's perfectly healthy for a man to devour a cake every now and then."

"And take thirds at every meal, too." Georgia set plates, forks, and napkins on the table.

"Are you serious?" Eliza asked. "How do you stay fit?"

He leaned back and patted his tummy. "Ah, that's the best part. My brain works so quickly, it completely energizes the rest of me. My metabolism is like a fifteen-year-old boy's most of the time."

"You know, that explains so much more than you realize." She turned to a laughing Georgia. "How can I help you?""

"Keep getting Will. You have no idea how much fun it is to have a sister around who can clobber him."

Eliza's brain skittered to a halt at the word "sister." Thankfully the two continued on without her.

"Whatever. She isn't clobbering anything. She's too tiny."

Georgia began to slice the cake. "Don't let him fool you. He's shaking in his boots."

"Socks. Remember, I'm wearing socks."

"Fine. Socks. But you're still shaking." She handed a piece of cake to Eliza.

"If I'm shaking, it's because of low blood sugar. What's taking so long?"

"Hush. Now how big do you want your piece?"

Eliza took a bite of hers. Suddenly every distracted thought she had of becoming Georgia's sister fled. "Oh, my gosh. Will, take a huge one. You're going to want it."

"You heard the lady. Gimme one huge slice."

Eliza quickly took another bite. She didn't care if she was talking with her mouth full. "Georgia, this is seriously to die for. I need the recipe. Like, must. Have. It."

"Careful. If it's that good, you might actually die." Will took the plate his sister handed him and dug in.

"Have I ever mentioned how charming you are?" Eliza took another bite.

"Well, she could've poisoned us. You never know. Huh, sis?" He looked up at her.

Georgia sat down and shook her head. "As tempting as it is to kill you, Will, I have yet to give in to the urge."

"Aw, it's so nice to have a sister who loves me."

Eliza put her fork down. "Good grief, you're incorrigible today. What's with you?"

He gave his best innocent face. "Aren't I always like this?"

Both girls shook their heads.

"I think he's showing off," Georgia stage-whispered.

"I think he really needs to read one of my books— perhaps get some tips on flirting."

Will threw his head back and laughed.

Georgia grinned and took a bite of cake. "Do you really think it's good?"

"Yes. Holy, yes. It's wonderful. You are really, really talented." Eliza took another bite. "Did you make this from scratch?"

The girl blushed and looked down. "Yeah."

"There's no way I could come close to this. The best cake I make is with a box—anything from scratch turns out super heavy and dry. This is just perfect. Where'd you get all the stuff to make it?"

"Thank you. Will had the hotel bring up the ingredients for me."

She should've known. "You should open up your own shop. Have you ever considered it?"

"I've thought about it, sure. But I've kind of given up on the idea. Do you think I should open one?

"And you're completely self-taught? No schooling?"

The girl shook her head. "None."

"Incredible. You were born to bake." Eliza leaned forward. "Okay, look. I know you're still young, so to make this work, your best bet is to get a business degree. That way, you understand the numbers side of all this. And then I'll come and help you put together a killer marketing plan, and I'll glance over the place and guarantee you keep your sales up high."

Georgia's eyes sparkled. "Do you really think I could get away with this?"

"Not only do I think you can do it, but I bet if your brother helped you out with some of his skills and contacts, you'll be running your own cake-making business and selling them to restaurants and stores. All you need is one good-sized chain to pick you up, and bam! You're not just a small corner shop—everyone in America gets to experience this masterpiece."

"Oh, wow! You really think I'm *that* good?"

Eliza took another bite. "You're awe-inspiring. Do you have a name picked out already? It'd have to be something killer. Something that'll make people take notice and remember."

"Actually, I do." Georgia grinned and then glanced away. "Okay. So, no one knows this, but I have a whole notebook full of ideas and notes and recipes for a shop one day."

"So you really have been thinking about it."

"Yeah." Georgia grinned. "I have some of my ideas on the iPad you brought. You wanna see them?" She stood up and headed toward her bedroom.

"Sure." Eliza set her fork down. As she stood, she caught sight of Will across the table. He had leaned back and was watching her. She couldn't quite read his expression. "Er, is it okay if I talk with Georgia about opening her own store?"

"You mean, give her hope? A dream? Something to live for? And someone to become?" He slowly stood up. "Eliza, I don't know what I've done to you. I imagine— knowing me and my innate idiocy—it was something awful. But if you could ever find it in your heart to forgive me, I would love to—"

"Eliza, are you coming?" Georgia called from the bedroom. "Or should I bring the iPad out there?"

Her eyes never left Will's. "I'm coming." There was so much there she really wasn't equipped to deal with right now. Rescuing Georgia was what this was all about. Wasn't it?

"Whatever it is, I'm so sorry," he said. "Please forgive me."

That night, holding Jane while she sobbed, collided with the image of Will across the table. She shook her head. "We'll talk later. Not now. Later."

He nodded. "Okay."

Eliza stepped away, her heart clenching as she made her way to the bouncing Georgia.

"Sorry, it's charging, so it's over here by the chair," the girl said. She beckoned Eliza to the side of the room. "I really want to show you my designs and maybe get your opinion on the name. I know you like chocolate, but wait until you see this one." She held up the iPad. On the screen was an incredible carrot cake, with toasted coconut on the sides.

"Wow. And this is from scratch too?"

She beamed. "Yep." Pushing her finger across the screen, Georgia popped the next picture up. "Scroll through them all. I have something like fifteen different cakes and seven cheesecakes, as well as cookies, pies—everything."

"This is amazing." Georgia had already begun a portfolio.

She happily sighed and sat down on the bed. "Yeah, actually, my boyfriend told me he'd help me open my own shop, so I was getting stuff ready for it."

All at once, they were treading on very dangerous ground. "You have a boyfriend? Does he like cakes too?"

Her smile slipped, and she looked away. "That's right, no—I don't have a boyfriend now. That was before. Back when we were thinking about getting married."

"Wow. Marriage. That's exciting." Eliza couldn't imagine any man taking advantage of such a sweet girl, let alone leading her along like this, only to destroy her.

She shrugged, and a visible frown showed up. "I thought so too. Turns out, it's really not that great after all."

Eliza cautiously sat down next to her on the bed, one arm going around those fragile shoulders. "Hey, it's okay, sweetie. I was engaged once."

"You were?"

"Yep. Turns out he was a jerk. I know exactly how you feel."

CHAPTER TWENTY-ONE:

"What was his name? Georgia asked.

Eliza closed her eyes and pushed through the hurt that came with him. "Collin."

"Do you mind talking about him? If you do, we can stop." The girl looked so lost, so alone, so eager to connect with her.

Only Jane had heard the full story of Collin. After all these years she wasn't sure she could open up so easily. But if it would help ease Georgia's pain… "Of course. Ask whatever questions you'd like."

"How old were you?"

How old *was* she? It happened so long ago, she'd almost forgotten. "Not much older than you. Maybe nineteen."

"Were you in love?"

Eliza nodded, her heart growing cold. "I thought so. I thought I knew everything there was to know about love— I was wrong."

"What'd he do?"

Taking a deep breath, Eliza leaned back and stretched her legs out in front of her. "What didn't he do?" She attempted a half chuckle. "I don't know. Collin was—Collin was so caught up in himself, he never saw me."

Georgia nodded, but didn't say anything.

"He wanted to be famous. And rich. And live in a huge house. Basically everything you guys are—he wanted it. And he literally brown-nosed his way through life to get there. Complimenting people he wanted to be like, lavishing praise on them. As for me, he was always worried about appearance, afraid of what others thought of him—of us. Constantly nagging, belittling, degrading." She took another deep breath. "It was one of those emotionally abusive relationships that scar. Those scars run deep. I'm sort of afraid of anyone who has that mentality now. I know how badly they cut you. It's hard when your partner doesn't find you desirable. There comes a point when you try anything to be another person—you forget who you are just so they're happy. Believing this is best for you, that they're bringing out the real you.

"But it's not the real you. It's a façade of lies they created. And eventually, those lies begin to eat you whole. Collin never even looked back when I finally left. He was engaged just a couple of weeks later to another girl we both knew. I've always felt sorry for her, honestly."

Eliza began to fiddle with the skirt of her dress. "He broke me a lot worse than I thought. I thought I was the strong one because I walked away. I thought I'd healed, and that was the worst hurdle."

She touched her chest over her heart. "No. It had only just begun. My journey of finding me after that fiasco took years of growing. And trusting. And believing I was worth it and good enough. It didn't help that my mom loved Collin, and she was livid that I'd hurt him the way I did. For months afterward, she'd still mutter under her breath about how disappointed she was that I hadn't married him.

I was a failure in her eyes, and it put a serious strain on our relationship."

"So did that girl marry him?"

"Charlotte? Yeah, they were married really fast. Within a couple of months or so. And as far as I know, they're still married."

"I wonder if my ex-boyfriend will get married soon."

Eliza decided to push a bit. "What's his name?"

"George, which was kinda cool because mine's Georgia. But he went by Joe."

Even though Eliza knew the answer, she had to ask. "How'd you meet? School?"

"No. He's older than me, so he'd already graduated from college. We originally found each other on Facebook. He started liking my posts and told me I inspired him, and yadda, yadda, yadda. I believed everything he said. And then, when we met, it was romantic and he was totally hot, and I completely forgot about the age difference. He just looked so young, it didn't matter. And I couldn't believe he'd actually fallen for me. Out of all the girls he was friends with on Facebook and Instagram and Snapchat—and he had a lot—he chose me. It totally went to my head.

"He took me on long walks in the park, to the zoo, hiking in the mountains—anywhere you can imagine that's romantic and perfect and unique and fun, he took me there. Then a few weeks ago, he proposed." She exhaled and stood up, but didn't stop talking. "He got down on one knee and told me there had never been a girl so beautiful and inspiring and right for him. He told me how happy I made him, and how he couldn't wait to show me the world and be my husband."

Tears started to form in her eyes, and Eliza's heart dropped. She knew that happiness—that joy. And then to have it destroyed so savagely. It wasn't fair.

Georgia wiped at her eyes. "Like a fool, I believed every word. I loved him so, so much. I knew—I just knew my world would be perfect, and he'd always take care of me." She walked to the door and laid her head against it.

"I couldn't wait to introduce him to Will. I was positive my brother would love him as much as I did." She sighed. "I was so stupid. I should've known then, when he said he didn't want to meet my family yet. I should've seen the signs. I should've known what he was and that he was hiding, that he was scared of Will and was hoping to—was hoping to..." She trailed off. Slowly, she turned around and slid down the door to land in a puddled heap on the floor.

Eliza walked toward her, and Georgia instantly tucked her knees up to her face and buried her head in them. Eliza sat next to her on the carpet and wrapped one arm around her shoulders.

"Shh... It's okay. You're safe now. I promise he won't hurt you again."

"Why?" Georgia sobbed. "Why? What did I ever do except love him? Why would he hurt me so much?"

"Come here." Tears sprang to Eliza's eyes as she gently tugged on the girl's shoulder. Georgia tucked herself into Eliza's lap and cried.

"I was so scared. I was so alone. And he was s—so mean. Just evil. He took everything from me. Everything." Her poor, frail shoulders shook beneath Eliza's hand. "I was too afraid to call Will and tell him what happened. And I was so ashamed of myself for being so stupid."

"You weren't stupid. It wasn't your fault."

She wiped her eyes and nodded her head. "Oh, yes, it was. This was *my* fault. Yes, I know George Wickham is a malicious, *vile* man—I know what he is! And I don't blame myself for the monster that he is and will be forever. No, may he die in prison for what he's done to me. And he will.

My brother will make sure he does. But *no*. My stupidity is because I trusted him. My blind, awful trust. I tossed aside any bad feelings I had, all that I'd been taught, and like an idiot, I followed him blindly.

"Eliza, I thought I would die that night. I thought he would actually kill me. Then he threatened to k—kill anyone I told. He took everything—my wallet, my phone, my suitcases, my jewelry—even the engagement ring. And then left me in the horrid hotel room—he laughed at me as he left. Calling me the worst names. And then I didn't see him again."

"I'm so sorry." Eliza held Georgia close again as she gently tried to comfort her. "What did you do?"

"I was so scared and ashamed and mortified. I stayed in the room for two days and cried. By the time I realized how hungry I was, I'd begun to wake up to the reality of what really happened. He'd left me in the room with nothing, but thankfully, he'd used my credit card to sign us in. We'd originally planned to be there a week, so I knew the reservation was for that long. When they didn't kick me out, I realized that Joe had forgotten about canceling the reservation. So I stayed in the room and ordered food service while I tried to decide what to do." She took a deep breath and sniffed.

"By then, I was beyond mad and I was ready to fight Joe with all I had. I'd come out of the haze enough to see what was really going on. But by the time I went to call Will and finally figured out what I would say to him, he walked in with the hotel security guards and saved me."

CHAPTER TWENTY-TWO:

Eliza and Georgia talked and wept and talked for another two hours before Eliza convinced her it was time for bed. Once she'd tucked her in, Eliza yawned and walked out. It had been one long day, and she was simply exhausted. There on the couch, still dressed in his clothes from the date and Ghostbusters socks, was Will. He was sound asleep and snuggled into an accent pillow. For a moment, she stared at his sweet, unguarded face and marveled at the man in front of her. He was Georgia's hero. For the last couple of hours, it was all Eliza had heard— how wonderful he was.

It was unbelievably kind of him to let them talk and bond while he obviously still waited for her to come back out. He was patient. That simple act showed wisdom and love beyond what she imagined.

She sat down on the couch opposite his and began to put her shoes back on. Then she walked over and gave him a gentle kiss on the cheek. "Goodnight."

His hand snaked out and grabbed hers before she could leave. "Wait," he said groggily. "Let me wake up so we can talk a minute." He groaned and sat up, rubbing his eyes.

"Will, it's okay. We can talk in the morning. You're asleep and I'm exhausted. But I didn't want to leave without saying a quick good-bye."

He yawned again, still rubbing his eyes. Ignoring her request, he asked, "How is she?"

She paused a moment and then gave in. "Good. She's going to sleep now."

He nodded. "What time is it?"

"I don't know." Eliza couldn't resist and yawned too. "Last I looked, it was close to midnight, but that was a while ago."

"Did she tell you anything?"

"Yeah, everything." She kneeled down on the floor next to him. "We had a really nice bonding moment. And hopefully, I've set her on the right path to heal."

"Thank you." He looked so out of it.

"No problem. She's an awesome girl. Really bright and fun and…"

Will blinked and actually looked at her for the first time. Then his hands captured her face and slowly and gently, he kissed her, his soft lips connecting with hers in a powerful gift of thanks. "You have no idea what this means to me." He kissed her again. "I knew if I gave her some time with you, you'd fix it."

Eliza's heart was hammering, and all at once, she was very much awake. "I don't know if I fixed anything…"

He touched her forehead with his and whispered, "Shh… You are miraculous."

This intimate nearness, the caring voice whispering deeply—it was a trap to tug at her heartstrings and keep her next to him forever. "Will?"

"Hmm?" Slowly, his hands moved from her jaw down her neck to rub her weary shoulders.

Oh, my goodness. Nothing had ever felt so good. She leaned forward and allowed his hands to work their magic.

"Turn around, and I'll get these kinks out for you."

She didn't need to be asked again. She turned around and Will began to knead and coax the stress away. "You are a magician."

He chuckled. "Oh, you deserve so much more than this."

She held her breath for a second before grinning and relaxing into his hypnotic trance. "Please don't stop. I may just fall asleep right here, but whatever you do, don't stop."

"Gladly. I'll keep you here forever just massaging your back." His strong, lean fingers began to run up the sides of her neck, along her spine, very cautiously working out the kinks under her hair.

"Oh…" Eliza was in heaven.

"So, how did you get my extremely private and proud sister to open up to you?"

The tightness slowly began to melt. There was only a very small part of her that was coherent. It took a minute for his question to make sense in the putty in her brain. "Georgia? Oh, I just told her about my failed engagement, and then we connected."

His hands stilled.

"Oh, please don't stop." She probably sounded like a baby, but it'd been years since anyone had rubbed her neck, and it felt so wonderful.

"What engagement?" he asked, his voice a bit huskier than before as he began to massage again.

She lolled her head forward. "It was just this guy I thought I was in love with. Collin. Found out we weren't in love, so I ended the engagement."

"How'd you find out? Did he cheat on you?"

Giggling a bit deliriously, she answered, "No." She sighed. "That feels so great."

"What did he do?"

"He was an emotionally abusive wreck, and he took it out on me and made me believe his way of thinking was the only one." She shrugged. "I really don't want to talk about it."

"I'm sure you don't." His thumbs began to make small circles at the base of her skull.

She honestly thought she'd succumb to bliss. "Ahhh…"

"What did he say to you?"

Eliza frowned. "I don't want to talk about it."

"I know. What did he say?"

"Everything."

"Like?"

"That I looked bad in certain outfits, and my hair was awful, and I needed makeup, and I wasn't saying the right things to the wealthy people he knew." She yawned again. "His whole goal was to become rich and live this snobbish lifestyle and be everything that made me lose me. Nothing was good enough, and nothing would ever be."

"So he basically said everything I said to you those first few months of working for me."

"Yep. You were a jerk."

His hands moved down to her shoulders. "So you were in love with a man who told you that you weren't good enough or pretty enough, and spent his whole time freaking out over what others thought of him and you."

"Yeah."

"And it slowly began to eat you alive until you lost sight of you. And then you eventually had to leave or you'd cease to exist."

How had he pieced that all together? Her fuzzy mind became a bit more awake. "You've been there?"

"Oh, yeah."

"Who?"

"My dad. Old girlfriends I've had. But mostly my dad."

She wrapped an arm around one of his legs that were straddling her as she sat on the floor in front of him. "Oh, Will, I'm so sorry."

His fingers pulled back. "I'm sorry I acted like him when we met."

She took a deep breath and turned around. "Me too."

He stared at her for some time. Those dark chocolate eyes looked so stricken and lost. As if he couldn't believe he'd mirrored what she was afraid of most in men. "So this is why you turned me down, isn't it?"

Her chest tightened. "Yes."

"After all you'd been through, the last thing you needed was another man who wanted his own personal Barbie doll."

The reality of his words hit home harder than she thought they would. "Please, let's talk about this later." She didn't know how much longer she'd be able to hold on.

"Eliza, you only came to help me. From the moment you stepped into that office, your goal was to make me a better man, a better CEO, and give my company astronomical growth and sales. That was your objective. You are a healer—an angel who can guide and uplift and give back only good."

Her breathing became more shallow, yet she couldn't look away from him. Finally, someone understood. Someone saw beneath her strong exterior.

"And I . . . I was a spoiled, selfish brat who'd gone too long doing things my own way. I didn't want to hear what you had to say. I was afraid you were right. So instead, I mocked you and belittled you, and attempted to drag you down. But you didn't falter. You gained my admiration and respect and eventually love because you knew I needed you. You saw potential and you stuck it out, despite the pain I caused. You have more integrity than anything I've ever known in my life."

He blinked and looked away, his hand rubbing above his eyes. "Of course you turned me down. It was the smart thing to do. Even a few days ago, I didn't fully understand who I was proposing to." Pulling out his phone, he continued, "If it's after midnight, it's been one week since that night. There's so much I wouldn't have understood if you'd said yes."

"Will, don't... It's okay."

He shook his head. "No, let me say this. I should at least own this much. I loved you, yes. But I loved you because of all you did for *me*." His shoulders shook, and he inhaled a shaky breath. "Don't you see? Even after all I put you through earlier, even after the junk you've found out about me, you are still here. Why? Because I needed you. Because you are still the good, incredible woman you are. I'm afraid I would've always taken advantage of that."

And there lay the mockery of her life. "You are wrong, Will. You wouldn't always have taken advantage of me. I never fully understood you either. And if I'd said yes, it would've been for the wealth, the advantages you could've given me. The power—the exact things I say I despise most. I couldn't marry you. I can't ever marry you because then I'll become the person Collin wanted me to be."

"The rich powerful person you've always secretly wished you could be?"

"Yes." One small tear released. "The one person I'm afraid of most."

"You, snobbish and critical and selfish?" "Yes."

CHAPTER TWENTY-THREE:

"I can't become her, Will. I can't. Then this angel you've fallen for won't exist anymore."

He shook his head, but he was wise enough not to disagree with Eliza. He could see that she was completely wiped out, and too hard on herself to believe in a happier world at the moment. "Okay. Let's get you to bed." He grinned slightly at her confusion. "I meant let's get you to your hotel room, where you can sleep."

"I will punch you if I need to." She closed her eyes.

"And she's back." He stood up and held his hand out for her. "It's time we end this heaviness for right now anyway."

She groaned. "Why do all the worst subjects come up late at night?"

"Probably because we're not coherent enough to avoid them."

"I hate it when you're right."

He tugged on her hand and pulled her to her feet. Then, because everything about her was too adorable not to, he wrapped her up in his arms and gave her a bear hug—just placed that ornery head against his chest and allowed her world to center a bit.

He felt her arms wrap around his waist as she snuggled in closer. She smelled so good. He held her like that for a few minutes, just rocking gently back and forth until eventually, she completely melted. Then he knew he'd better get her to her room before she fell asleep on her feet.

In an odd moment of chivalry, he swooped her up in his arms, cradling her like he would a child, and began to walk out the door.

"Will, put me down. I can walk." Eliza yawned and rested her head on his shoulder.

He pushed the button of the elevator and walked in. "I swear, you'd protest food after being stranded on a deserted island."

"But I *can* walk."

"Uh-huh. I'll bet. Now be quiet and let someone think of you for a change." Tapping her floor number, he leaned back against the wall and waited.

"You're so bossy." She held on to his shirt and tucked her head against his neck.

Her warmth breath splayed just under his ear, wreaking all sorts of havoc. "Well, I am your boss. I think I'm allowed to be."

She chuckled softly, creating those sensations again, and he nearly dropped her as the doors opened.

"You're not the boss of me."

"Okay, princess. I'm going to need you to be quiet now." If not, he wasn't sure he'd make it to the door.

"I'm not a princess."

"Right now you are."

"Nope." She yawned. "That would make you a prince, and you're no prince."

He grinned. "Touché." Even half asleep, she never let up. Where had she been his whole life? And how had he seen only see half of her awesomeness? He let loose a long breath. There needed to be a plan. Something to completely derail where they were headed now.

He had to think of a way to get her to see how good she really was, so she knew without a doubt that she wouldn't change once they were together.

His breath caught in his throat at the thought. Was he really hoping to have a second chance with her? To actually prove that they were meant to be together? How much of his pride was he willing to risk for this? Looking down her unguarded profile, he smiled slightly. All of it.

As he approached her door, he knocked. She wriggled in his arms. "Let me open it with the key in my purse."

"Uh, I don't think I brought it. Sorry."

"Will…"

"Yes?"

Just then, the door opened. "Oh, my goodness! What happened? Is she okay?" Melissa asked as she clutched her dressing gown and moved back to let Will carry her daughter in.

Eliza groaned and dropped her head onto his shoulder. "I'm fine, Mom."

"She's just sleepy." He winked at Melissa as he walked past.

Melissa giggled. "I'll let you help her to her room."

"I don't need help. Put me down—I'll be fine." Eliza moved, but he held on.

Melissa tsked. "No, she's not fine. She looks like a mess. Go ahead, Will, and do what you need to do."

"Mom! You're a turncoat."

He chuckled and walked into the bedroom. "Hey, be nice. You should listen to your mom."

"It's true. You should!" Melissa hollered back at them.

"You're going to have fun answering all the questions she'll have for you." He smirked.

"Nice. Something else I have to thank you for. Now, why can't I stop yawning?" she asked over yet another yawn.

"Probably because you're as exhausted as I say you are—you're just too stubborn to admit it."

"Said the king of stubborn," she mumbled into his shoulder. "So, are you going to put me down?"

"Debating it. Not sure yet." Truth was, it was absolutely wonderful to have her so close.

"Urgh. Why are you such a brat?"

"What?" He pretended to be shocked. "Are you really calling me a brat? Now if I was a brat, I'd do something like this." Without hesitating, he tossed her onto the bed.

"Oomph!" She gasped.

"There. You oughta be awake now." He swooped down, kissed her on her gaping mouth, and then walked out. "Night, darling. I'll see you in the morning."

Just as he shut the door, he heard a thump on the other side. "Hey! Was that your shoe?" he asked through the wood.

"Of course, you monster."

"Monster?" He opened the door and then quickly shut it again to let the other shoe hit. As soon as he heard the resounding bump, he whisked it open and pounced on the bed. "I'll show *you* monster. Now you're really gonna get it."

Eliza shrieked like a banshee, but he held her down on her back. "Did you honestly try to hit me in the head with your high-heeled shoe? And you have the audacity to call *me* a brat?"

"You deserved it!" She attempted to push at him and giggled. "You'd better let me go or I'm going to scream the place down."

"As soon as you open your mouth, I'll kiss you. So I'd rethink that if I were you."

The little beast opened her mouth and breathed as if to yell, and he captured it, kissing her. She pretended to protest as he gently released her arms, but they wound around him.

Melissa called from the doorway. "Just holler if you need me."

"Did you hear that?" he whispered against Eliza's mouth.

Melissa called out again. "That was for you, Will. You let me know if *you* need help."

They both chuckled just before he kissed her again.

After a few moments, she said, "Will?"

"Hmm?" He seriously would never get enough of these sweet lips.

"You need to stop."

"And why's that?" he murmured.

"Because I'm beginning to fall in love with you."

CHAPTER TWENTY-FOUR:

Will pulled back, his eyes searching Eliza's for a good full minute. She held her breath and silently chastised herself. Why would she say that to him? Why? She wasn't even sure where that had come from. Finally, he spoke.

"Okay. I'll stop and leave you alone. You need to catch up on your sleep anyway."

What? Mortification burned through her as she sat up and stammered. "I . . . uh . . . okay. Thanks for dinner."

"No problem." It was as if he was a different person altogether. "Thanks for talking to my sister." He kissed her cheek. "Well, I'm going to head out now. Hope you sleep well." And then he was gone.

She clutched the blanket to her chest as her heart dropped. Sure, she blurted out something she shouldn't have, but...? All at once, Eliza felt like crying. Everything around her seemed lonely and small. Her hands began to shake. Slipping under the covers, she curled herself into a ball and closed her eyes. Exhaustion crept its way into every inch of her. Why else would she feel the need to cry?

The next morning, Eliza slowly blinked awake. She could hear her mom humming some old song about going to the chapel and getting married. As soon as it registered what the melody was, she groaned and rolled over. Placing a pillow over her head, she lay there and debated the best course of action.

Today was Saturday. No, wait. They came to Vegas a day early. Today was only Friday, wasn't it? Her mind roamed over all that had happened the past twenty-four hours, and she became tired again just thinking of it. What time was it, anyway? She glanced around for her phone—no phone. Then she began to look for her purse. Were they in the front room? "Mom, what time is it?" she asked as loud as she could without yelling.

"What'd you need, sweetie?" Her mom came into the room. "Good morning, slugabed. So glad to see you're finally awake."

"What time is it?" she asked again, deciding it was best to address one issue at a time.

"Nearly one. Why?"

Eliza jolted up. "Are you kidding me? One p.m.? Holy . . . Mom! Why'd you let me sleep that late? Where's my phone?"

Her mom blinked. "Excuse me, but you clearly needed sleep."

"Not like twelve hours, though." She couldn't even remember the last time she'd gotten more than six hours of sleep. She glanced around the room again. Served her right for not having an alarm set on her phone. "I've practically wasted half the day. Good grief. So, do you know where my phone is?"

"Yes. Will called and said your purse and phone are still up in his suite."

She winced and flopped back on the bed. "Are you kidding me? I really don't want to see him today."

"All right. Enough with the drama." The bed bounced a bit as her mom got on it. "How dare you make that face when you were grinning just fine over the boy last night?"

"I don't want him to get the wrong idea."

"The wrong idea about what?" She tossed a pillow at Eliza. "Good grief. You're gonna run that man ragged if you pull this with him today."

"Pull what with him?"

She gestured toward her. "This. Exactly this."

"Which is?"

"You playing the victim. Enough. Get up and put a smile on your face, and you'd better tell that boy you love him and stop this foolishness."

She gasped. "Mom, for once and for all, I do not love Will Darcy."

"Liar." She scooted over a bit. "I shouldn't even be sitting here for fear your pants will catch on fire."

Eliza rolled her eyes and tried not to laugh. "I'm not in love with him."

"Bull. You've been in love with him for months. Now stop it."

"Stop being in love with him? Gladly. There. Done."

"You know what I mean."

"No, Mom. I don't." She sighed. "Please, explain, because obviously my words don't mean anything to you." She was embarrassed. She was frustrated. And she was ornery. This probably wasn't the best time to have this chat.

Her mom shook her head. "None at all. In fact, I don't even trust what comes out of your mouth anymore if this is what you're gonna wake up saying after allowing that man to kiss you senseless last night.'"

Her heart skipped a beat. "You saw that?"

Mom gave her the look. "Seriously? Were you even rational after his first kiss?"

She sighed. "Yes. I remember almost everything." She got quieter and plucked at the bedspread. "Even when I told him to stop kissing me because I was beginning to fall in love with him."

"Ah-ha!" Mom beamed. "I knew it. Oh, I'm so proud of you right now!"

Her stomach clenched. "Yeah, but I also remember that Will actually stopped kissing me after that and then he left." She tried to put her mouth into a smile, but it resisted.

"Hey, what's this?" Mom wrapped an arm around her. "Do you honestly think that man wanted to walk away from you?"

"What else am I to think?" She sighed. "I told him I was starting to fall in love with him, and he hightailed it out of here just as fast as he could."

"Elizabeth, he loves you. I know he does. I see it in every look he gives you."

She shook her head. "Not enough."

"Well, then, you should be pleased with yourself, and happy."

"What?" Eliza looked up. "What do you mean?"

Her mom shrugged. "It was this side of a week ago you were telling me how you couldn't stand him and you'd never like him. Well, there you go. Now you don't have to."

Scrunching over, Eliza put her head in her hands. "Is this some sort of reverse psychology thing? Because it isn't working."

"I'm just helping you see the bright side. Now all your dreams can come true."

"Look, I know what you're doing, and it's not going to work." Eliza fluffed a pillow behind her head and plopped down. "It doesn't even matter anyway because I still can't forgive him for what he did to Jane."

Mom sat up straight. "What did he do to Jane?"

"Oh, shoot. You didn't know about that, did you?" She sighed. "Nothing. Don't worry about it. It doesn't matter."

"Elizabeth Bennet, if you think for one minute that I'm going to let you simply brush this off, you're out of your mind. Now. I love Mr. Darcy. I think he's an amazing man. However, if he's done anything to hurt one of my girls, there is nothing that replaces that. Nothing. Now out with it. I want to know what happened."

"Mom, you don't."

"Now."

"Fine." Eliza got off the bed and stood up. "You know how Jane and Charles Bingley were dating?"

"The vice president of Revolutionary Innovations? Will's friend?"

"Yeah. The really nice one." Eliza picked up the fallen accent pillows and tossed them on the bed. Might as well quit stalling and just let her mom know the truth. She rubbed her lips together and took a deep breath. Her heart began to harden.

Her mom waited.

"Apparently, Will saw them together, and didn't think Jane really liked Charles."

"What?" Her mom looked stunned.

"So he told Charles that she was a gold digger, only after him for his money."

"Are you kidding me?" Mom looked like she was about to explode. "Of all the nerve!"

"So that's when everything screeched to a halt. Charles told Jane that he'd be too busy at work to date her, and walked away."

"Breaking my poor girl's heart."

Eliza nodded. "Yeah, I've never seen Jane cry like that before. I think she was more hurt and confused than anything. Had it been a natural break, it would've made sense. But to be treated as if she meant nothing to him just devastated her. Especially since she'd been wondering if he was the one."

Just then, someone knocked on the door.

"Hang on—I'll answer it. You're still in yesterday's dress." Mom headed toward the door and asked, "Who is it?"

"Melissa, it's Will. I've got Eliza's purse and phone."

Mom opened the door. "Good. Have a seat. You're just the man I was hoping to see."

CHAPTER TWENTY-FIVE:

Eliza could hear her mother begin to grill Will, and like the wimp that she was, she decided now would be a good time to take a shower. She closed her bedroom door. No reason for them both to jump on the poor guy.

After she was all clean and dressed in jeans and a T-shirt, she removed the towel from her hair and began to scrub it dry when she heard a light tap on her door. "Come in," she called.

Will peeked his head in. "Hey, do you mind if we talk?"

"Sure."

He walked in and quietly shut the door.

"Let's sit on the comfy chairs." She pointed to the two high-backed chairs near the window. "Give me a second and I'll join you."

Will walked over and chose one without saying a word. Eliza busied herself with straightening the bed and then putting away her towels before joining him. Once she sat down, it was still a couple of minutes before he spoke.

She'd never seen him look so pensive.

Eventually, he let out a long breath. "So, it seems I owe you an apology."

She shook her head. "Not me, really. It's more for Jane."

His gaze collided with hers—she could tell he was absolutely miserable. "No. I owe you one first. This hurt you. I'm the sole reason for that, and I'm sorry. I never meant to cause you any pain."

Crossing one leg over the other, she leaned an elbow on the arm of the chair and looked at him, not ready to give in. Her heart was still too bruised from the night before. "Why did you do it?"

He sighed. "I was a fool. I . . . I had an issue with people only wanting my money, and I didn't want to see my friend fall blindly into a trap."

"Jane never would've expected anything from him."

"I know—your mom made that quite clear. I'm sorry, Eliza. I really am."

"I don't know what's more shocking—the fact that you put your nose between the middle of two adults having a relationship, or that you were so clueless to judge her harshly." She let out a smirk. "Me, sure. Judge me. That's fine. But Jane? The sweetest person on earth? Really?"

"These past few minutes, I've been trying to put myself in your shoes. What if someone had destroyed a relationship of Georgia's? One that she was finally able to have after all she's been through, and he was a great guy. What would I've done to that person?" He rubbed the back of his neck. "Honestly, I'm surprised you've talked with me at all. Then, after learning about it, you still flew out here to help me. I don't deserve you."

"What was I supposed to do?" She closed her eyes. "Of course I would come help you. Of course I'd be there to support Georgia. We may have our differences, but what we disagree on will never lessen someone else's value."

"Yes, but while you so easily dropped everything and came to help my sister—without judging—I wasn't so kind. I not only had degrading thoughts about your sister, but I shared them with Charles. I figured I was right. Nothing was more important than my own opinions. Problem was, I ruined her so well that my ever-loyal and trusting friend eventually saw things my way and dumped her."

Eliza couldn't take anymore. She stood up. "Stop."

"I—I'm done. I'm sorry. I know this is painful."

Her hand shook, and she clutched the arm of the chair for balance. "It is painful. It's *too* painful. And after your reaction last night, I really don't think we need to talk about anything other than work. You've made it clear what you think of me and my sister. So let's change the subject. Do you have my phone? I'd like to check it for messages, to see if there's anything I need to do for the office today."

"Eliza…"

"I thought you had my phone. Where is it? With my mom?"

"Eliza, wait."

She put her hands on her hips. "What?"

"I love you too."

His words punched her in the gut so hard, she took a step back.

"I—what did you say?"

He stood up, holding his hands out. "I do. I still love you. Even more than when I first asked you to marry me a week ago."

"But last night … you left." She was so confused.

"I left so I wouldn't scare you. You have no idea how badly I wanted to shout and hold you and talk a hundred miles an hour. What I've been dying to do since I woke up so happy this morning. And I could barely contain myself enough to walk out the door last night. You were exhausted. You needed sleep. And I needed to calm down."

She blinked and slowly dropped her hands from her hips. "Really?"

"Yeah, really."

"But what does it mean?"

He chuckled. "Do you have any idea how adorable you look so confuzzled like that?"

"Confuzzled?"

"Yep. You are the definition of confuzzled." He began to walk toward her, taking very cautious steps. Once there, he gently held her just below her shoulders, then slid his hands down to capture her elbows. "Look, I know this is new and very fragile—and pretty much some serious thin ice right now, until I can make it up to Jane and Charles."

She gave a lopsided smile. "You would do that?"

"Why wouldn't I? I feel like an idiot right now. You have no idea."

One eyebrow rose. "You do realize that Jane and I are from the same family, right? I mean, weren't you worried that I was a gold digger too?"

"Ha. No. I knew better than to believe that of you. You'd have laughed in my face."

"Why do you say that?"

"Because I knew right away you weren't the type to be fooled by the greediness. You'd made it clear you found my lifestyle distasteful."

She nodded. "Always interjecting my ideas on where we should have business luncheons."

"Reminding me not to waste money." He shrugged. "It was because of you that I became more aware of how much I had wasted all these years. I began to save, and give more generously to charities than I'd given before."

"You mean like the women's shelter?"

"You knew?" He put his hands in his pockets. "You were always talking about women's shelters, so I thought if I'd donate to help their cause, it'd impress you and let you see I wasn't always about the money."

Wait a minute. "You did it to impress me?" Then why didn't she know about it until Jane said something?

"Yeah. That was the plan. Except when I got to the shelter and met with some of the people there, I realized how much they needed me. Well, my money."

"That's when you decided to pay for the rest of their remodeling?"

"That's when my purpose changed. It's when I decided this was so much more important than impressing you. This was women and children's lives and self-worth at stake."

"You're pretty much amazing."

He chuckled. "I was thinking the same thing about you."

Tilting her head to the side, she asked, "Now what?"

He grinned a small grin, as if he were afraid to. "I've been thinking about it, and I think we should do some fun stuff together in the next couple of days. Just see how things go. Take everything slow and steady and . . . just see."

She nodded. "I'd like that. Try to give this—us—some time to see if we actually fit as well as we think we might."

"Oh, you fit."

She blushed. "Good grief. Don't look at me like that!"

"Like what?" His eyes challenged hers to glance away. She didn't dare.

"Like I'm lunch."

"It's those lips. What can I say? I can't help it."

She giggled. "You know what?"

"Hmm?"

"You're the most aggravating, annoying, horrid man in all of the—"

He kissed her.

When she pulled away, she continued. "I can't believe the junk you've put me through. Seriously. I could write a book on what an—"

"I said I was sorry." He silenced her again. This time for much longer.

By time she released again, she sighed.

"Feel better?" He smiled.

She shook her head. "No. I think I'll need a few more."

Will laughed. "Gladly."

CHAPTER TWENTY-SIX:

They spent the rest of the day Friday just exploring the fun things to do in Vegas. It was the first time Georgia had been out on the town since she got there. Eliza's mom was more than game to throw ideas around as well. Will had his car take them to Ethel's Chocolate Factory and get their own private tour of the place—which was absolutely incredible. Eliza had never tried chocolate so delicious and fresh before. Then Melissa suggested that they visit the Botanical Cactus Gardens next door.

They each carried a small bag of their favorite chocolates and walked over to the gardens. Eliza's mom insisted on teaching them about the different cacti and their purpose in the desert environment.

"Your mom really knows her cactuses." Will nudged Eliza's shoulder as he came up next to her.

"Cacti," she whispered. "And yeah, she does. Don't get her started on the flowers that grow in Utah or we'll never leave."

"I don't mind, actually. It's really kind of cool just to be here, outside, with you." He popped a chocolate in his mouth and then easily slid his hand into hers. She loved the feel of his strong larger hand wrapped around hers.

Georgia grinned as she came up to them, her eyes definitely noticing the linked couple. "So, do you two have something you want to tell me?" She beamed from one to the other.

"About what?" Will grinned.

"Ahem." Georgia tucked her arm through her brother's. "You know, anything exciting about the two of you that'll make me totally eager to begin planning, say—I don't know—a bridal shower or something?"

Eliza rolled her eyes. "Oh, no, not you too. You're as bad as my mom."

"Hey!" Melissa hollered. "No wedding plans until Will gets out of the dog house. Period."

"What?" He acted shocked. "This isn't enough?"

Her mom flipped her short curls and lifted up her sunglasses. "Are you kidding me, boy? I'm expecting one heck of a birthday. And gifts. Did I mention gifts?" She tapped her foot. "And they're not your typical lavish fanfare, either. I mean, one happy Eliza and a very delighted Jane oughta give you a bit more room to talk."

Will threw his head back and laughed. "Duly noted. Though, what if I'd like to send a few lavish gifts your way—would you accept?"

She tsked. "Of course I would. Do I look like a fool?" Flicking at her earlobes, she said, "I prefer sapphires."

"She has no shame." Will laughed.

"None at all." Eliza tugged at his hand. "You're better off not encouraging her."

"I heard that," Melissa said as she toddled off toward a beautiful section of flowering cacti with her large white purse in the crook of her elbow. "Come here, Georgia, and tell me which ones are your favorites."

They waited until Georgia headed off before Will stopped and looked down at Eliza. "She's pretty amazing."

"Who? My mom?"

"Yep. When we were chatting earlier—er, more like when she was chewing me out about Jane—she mentioned that this past year, she's been trying to get you to see me. She realized we'd be perfect for each other the moment you told her about your first awful day of work."

Eliza nodded. "It's so true. She's been hounding me about you nonstop ever since."

"Hey, what's that face? I love that she's like that!"

"You do?" Was the guy insane?

"Of course. As long as it's me she's trying to set you up with, I'm one-hundred percent in on any and all shenanigans she comes up with."

She chuckled. "You would be."

"Do you blame me?" Will kissed her, right there in the Las Vegas sunshine.

With each new kiss, Eliza's world centered a bit more. She became that much closer to believing in this surreal reality. Eliza Bennet was actually kissing Will Darcy in a garden in Vegas. There were some things that needed to be repeated over and over in her mind before she could believe they were actually true.

When he pulled back, he brushed a strand of hair from her face. "You have no idea what kissing you does inside me."

She looked at him funny and chuckled. "What do you mean?"

"I don't know. This must be what a teen girl feels like after her crush asks her to dance."

Eliza laughed. "I honestly have to say, that is the most disconcerting thing I've ever heard come out of your mouth!"

"What? It's true, though. It feels all giddy and girly and weird."

"I'd stop while you're ahead. This is only getting creepier."

He shook his head. "Man, I've needed you. You'll never be afraid of me, will you?"

"No." She looked toward her mom and his sister and then back over at him. His eyes searched hers as the clenching in her heart tightened. She didn't realize until that moment. "The only thing I'm afraid of is losing you." And she meant it. Every word.

He nodded, his face matching hers in their sudden moment of seriousness. "I know exactly what you mean." They stared at each other, absorbing it all, before Will glanced over at the other two and broke the spell. "How do you think your mom is holding up? I was hoping to take Georgia to the indoor amusement park, but we can do that tomorrow."

"Yeah, I don't know. I think Mom will be a lot more tired than she lets on. Let's save the park for tomorrow and take her to dinner and then to a symphony or off-Broadway show. Do you know of any that have seats available?"

He fished in his pocket and pulled out tickets to see Disney's Newsies or the London Pop Orchestra, both that night, each of them during the same time and in different casinos.

"Will? You didn't!"

He shrugged. "I couldn't risk them being sold out, so I bought exclusive seats for each. Then I figured I'd let you guys decide."

Did he think of everything? "I can't wrap my head around this."

"Oh, and I've got tickets for both of them tomorrow night too, just in case you girls couldn't choose."

She kissed him for his craziness. But mostly she kissed him for his thoughtfulness. He'd chosen the two perfect performances for their group—nothing risqué or loud or showy, proving that his guests were incredibly important to him. And what man thinks like that? Who does that? "I love you."

"Yes!" He grinned and then kissed her again. "That's twice today." He waggled his brows. "Ten times, and you get a treat."

She laughed. "I'm afraid to ask."

"You don't get to know. Not until you've earned it."

"Ha! Well, who's to say you'll earn ten 'I love you's' from me?"

"That's three!" he exclaimed as he stole another kiss.

After taking them to a sampler buffet dinner, they chose *Newsies* for the first night. He dropped the girls off in time to get all dolled up again and then back out to the show. There were new songs, and the acting, choreography, everything, was brilliant! Eliza loved the excitement in the air, the extra buzz that energized the whole room whenever live theater took place. It was simply exhilarating.

However, about two scenes in from the second act, Will received a text.

After reading it, he passed the phone over to Eliza.

They'd found Joe. He was gambling at a casino right then. The owner had agreed to keep him in the area, making sure he stayed right where he was—which meant, keeping him winning—until Will could get there.

She looked at him in the middle of a flashy song and said, "Let's go."

CHAPTER TWENTY-SEVEN:

Will passed the phone to Georgia and Melissa. After reading it, they waited until the scene ended before getting up and leaving the theater.

"Okay, I'm going to drop you three off in front of the hotel and then head to the other casino. Is that all right?" Will asked as they got into the car.

"Are you out of your mind?" Eliza was appalled.

All three women complained.

"Wait a minute. Are you saying you want to be there when we get Joe?"

"Yes!" Georgia sounded ticked. "I—out of anyone— deserve a chance to see him get arrested!"

"She's right, Will. Why would you even think of dropping us off?" Melissa buckled her seat belt. "Take us to the casino."

"You too, eh?" He turned to Eliza.

"You'd better believe it." She snapped her seat belt in place. "I wouldn't miss this for the world."

"Then I have officially been outnumbered. On to get Joe."

"Yes!" Eliza's mom exclaimed. "Let's do this thing."

Will had the car parked at the back of the casino. Guards were waiting to escort them through the kitchens to the front. The private investigator and owner met them just before they made it to the main lounge. Both men were chatting excitedly.

"He's at the craps table, and winning a good chunk of change. Two of the people he's playing against are our guys. And he's just picked up a girl who's working with us too. We're holding out until you see him. We've got cameras for documentation and anything you may need in court…"

Eliza listened for a second before noticing a collection of people also coming out of the woodwork, dressed as guests, but clearly they were with the owner.

Will caught Eliza's eye and explained, "They're private security. They've just showed up. This lounge is crawling with them, just in case he tries to bounce."

It was one of the coolest things she'd ever witnessed, almost like they were in the movie *Ocean's Eleven* or something. Her adrenaline began to accelerate the closer they got to the table.

"There he is." The P.I. pointed to the back of a man in a dark suit.

"I see him." Will's face looked grim.

Eliza touched his elbow. "Are you okay?"

"Oh, I've never been better." He turned around. "Now, I want you ladies to blend into the background. You can watch, but I don't want any of you getting hurt. Do you understand?"

When no one nodded, he tossed his hands in the air. "Guys. Seriously. This is for real now. I have no idea if he's armed or what—or what he'll do once he realizes he's been caught. Just promise me he won't notice you. Okay?"

"Fine." Eliza looped her arms through her mom's and Georgia's elbows. Together, they began to walk around the area, still heading toward Joe's table, but situating themselves at another one to the left.

Then they watched as Will walked up to Joe, the men discreetly staying behind. He tapped Joe on the shoulder, and Eliza chuckled as the other man scrambled to his feet. He was as white as a ghost. His eyes darted from side to side, as Will was clearly telling him off.

Joe threw his dice on the ground, and several men stepped forward and held him by the arms. Over the roar of the casino, Eliza could barely hear Will's threats as they handcuffed and searched Joe.

"I don't care what he says," Georgia grumbled as she stomped toward him. "I'm giving that moron a piece of my mind!"

"Georgia, wait!" Eliza ran after her.

"Will's going to kill us!" Her mom giggled behind them both.

Eliza held Melissa back as Georgia walked right up to her ex and then punched him in the face. Hard. "Don't you ever speak to me again!"

Eliza winced as the girl shook her hand in obvious pain.

"I wish I knew she was about to do that," Mom sniggered. "I could've gotten her a crow bar and saved her the broken hand."

But a broken hand wasn't about to stop her. She wasn't done yet. "My brother and I are going to make sure you rot in jail! Then you'll know real pain!" Georgia slammed her foot into Joe's groin before a few men grabbed her and pulled her back. "You'll pay for everything you did to me!"

Joe went down with tears in his eyes while Georgia continued to shout at him.

The ruckus was beginning to draw a crowd. The owner nodded to a few of his men, and everyone moved to the back as soon as possible so the gaming could commence.

As Eliza followed behind, she could hear the chuckling respect of a couple of the undercover security—they were pretty impressed with Georgia.

"And then that girl just whacked him as hard as she could in the jewels. I thought I'd die of laughter right then."

"I don't know, man. When that ball of fury advanced, I knew the pretty boy wouldn't have a face left."

"Serves him right, the perv."

Will approached as they entered into the large back room. "Hey, I'm going to have the car brought over. The cops are on their way. I want you and Melissa and Georgia to head back to the hotel. I've got a lot of stuff I have to go through with the police, and I really don't want Georgia to see this junk. Can you keep an eye on her?"

They shared a look. She understood exactly what he couldn't say out loud with so many people around— Georgia shouldn't be left alone. No matter how brave she was now, this was going to hit, and it'd hit hard. He needed her as far away from Joe as she could get for the time being.

"Okay. She'll be with us in our suite."

A look of relief passed over his features. "Thank you." He leaned forward and kissed her. "I know this isn't how we planned to spend the evening, but I feel a ton better knowing he's been caught."

Eliza nodded. "Me too."

"Oh, and here." He reached into his suit pocket and pulled out money. "I'll call and have the hotel doc look at her hand. If it's bad, here's the money you'll need to take her to the ER. Hopefully, it's just bruised."

"Yeah." She made a face. "That looked so painful for them both."

He shook his head. "I didn't see it coming, but it sure made me proud. I kind of think it was totally worth the pain—on her part."

"She's definitely feisty."

He got a text. "Okay. The car's waiting out back. I'll see you in a few hours."

She didn't want to leave him. Every part of her begged to stay there. "I love you. Be safe."

He grinned and kissed her again. "That's four. I love you too. Now go. I'll be there soon. Text me when you know about her hand."

CHAPTER TWENTY-EIGHT:

Way after Georgia's hand was fixed and Eliza's mom had fallen asleep in her bed and Georgia had tucked herself to sleep in Eliza's bed, Eliza lay awake on the couch in the living room waiting for Will. Part of her problem was that she'd slept in so much earlier, but the other problem was this dang excitement coursing through her.

She felt alive and curious to see what was coming next, as if this chapter in her life was finally closing, and soon the buzz she felt in the air would belong to her. Could he really love her? Could they actually make this work?

She grinned and stretched and wiggled her toes and thought about the past year of her life with Will Darcy. Everything really did seem to come alive once he came into the picture. Even though she mistook the attraction for contention, her mom was probably right. She'd undoubtedly been steadily falling for the brat for months.

So this is what love was. This unbelievable urge to help when needed, to care for, and uplift, and worry over, and tease, and argue, and miss. It'd only been four or five hours, but she missed him.

As soon as she heard his knock on the door, she quickly got up to let him in. "Hi." She smiled.

Will looked haunted and exhausted, but he grinned when he saw her. "Hello, beautiful." He held his arms out as he walked in. "Come here."

She wrapped him up in a hug. "How did it go?"

"He's behind bars. Without bail. And will be there until the court date. It looks like Georgia and I will be back for court in a month or two, but I don't have to think about another thing for now."

"So do you know what damage he's done? How much he stole from you?"

"Hundreds of thousands, it looks like. We won't know until all the bills come in. Thankfully, he had a ton of cash stashed in his hotel room, so we'll be able to divvy that up throughout some of his debts, but I'm still out so much money, I don't even want to think about it."

"I'm so sorry. But at least he's behind bars and not hurting anyone else."

He sighed and slowly began to rub her back. "Oh, if only I could do this every single day."

"What?" Capture criminals? Was he joking?

"Come home to a warm hug from you."

"Oh." She snuggled in closer. "It is pretty nice, I have to admit." She stage-whispered, "Though I should probably let you know, we work together. And that means we'll be able to hug whenever we want."

"Every day. All day long." He began to move them around in a circle as if they were dancing.

She chuckled. "Dork."

"Come on—you don't think we could hold meetings like this? See? If we just turn around a bit, then voila! Just like one of my presentations."

"Let's try it on Monday." She reached up on tiptoes and kissed him. "What are they going to do, fire you?"

"That's what I'm talking about. This is why we're so perfect for each other."

"And I thought it was because I put you in your place."

He scrunched his nose. "Nah. That's why you're so good for me. But together, with these brilliant minds, we're practically unstoppable with so much awesomeness."

"All we need are capes."

"Hmm… You are pretty much a superhero in my book." He kissed along her cheek and jaw.

"That's because I'm so super."

"I'd rather think of it as magical."

"Ooh, you're right. I like that better. I'm magical." She sighed as his kiss moved to just below her ear. He was sending zings all over her. "Actually, I think you're more magical than me. I mean, these kisses—gah!"

He found her lips. "I love you, Ms. Elizabeth Bennet."

"Mmm… I love you too."

She felt him grin. "That's six."

"No, I didn't say I love you earlier. You're still at five."

"Fine. Now that's six."

Smiling in return, he began to sway and rock her in their miniature personal dance again. "Are you ever going to tell me what these ten 'I love you's' are about?"

"That's seven." He kissed her again.

"Will?"

"What?"

"Ugh. What does 'I love you' mean?"

"Eight."

"Oh, for crying out loud! I love you. I love you. There. Now I've said ten. What's my treat?"

"Ms. Elizabeth Bennet?"

"Yes? Are you going to tell me what my treat is?"

"I love you more than life itself. I would gladly die for you." "Okay? Thank you. But what does that have to do with what we're talking about?"

"Woman, hush. I'm trying to tell you right now. Now stop interrupting me."

"Did you just say 'woman'? As if I'm some sort of—"

"Yes. Now be quiet." He took a deep breath.

Her dad's advice rang loud and clear. Perhaps now was another good time to put that to use. She laughed. "I promise to be good. Go ahead."

"Actually, I've changed my mind."

"What?"

"I almost forgot. I can't give you your treat yet."

"Will, what in the world are you talking about?"

He pulled her into her bedroom and looked around until he spotted her laptop. "Here. First, you have to read the rest of that email. Then, I'll continue. That is, if you still want me to."

She hadn't thought of that email for at least a couple of days. "You're so lucky I love you. You know that, right?"

He nodded toward the computer. "Go ahead. I'll wait."

She gave him a funny look as she crossed over to the dresser and picked up the laptop. Then she crawled up on the bed and leaned against the headboard as she opened it. It took a couple of seconds before the email was in front of her again.

"Do you mind?" Will gestured toward the bed.

Eliza patted the area next to her. "Only if you promise to be quiet while I read it."

The bed shifted as he crawled over and joined her. He put one arm around her shoulder and tucked her back against his chest.

Together, they read.

CHAPTER TWENY-NINE:

Eliza quickly skimmed through the parts she'd already seen.

Elizabeth,

I've given it some thought, and I'd like to say you're right. Don't get me wrong—you're not right about everything. You're just right about a few things. Mainly my character. I was a jerk to you. I've treated you unkindly, and as I tried to explain earlier, unwisely. I felt from the beginning that having you come and help the company would look like I'd failed. How am I supposed to run such a large corporation when I'm not even qualified to know what's best for it?

There you were, in all your five-foot-two no-nonsense glory, and I was mad, definitely not wanting to be in the situation I'd been forced into, and definitely not wanting to pretend to be nice to you. As far as I could tell, you were too young, too attractive, and too much trouble for your own good. You spoke out of turn, you had no concept of the way we ran things, and you continued to criticize everything that had been achieved and put into place before you came along.

Yes, we argued a lot. It's something I came to respect about you—that you wouldn't take trash from me. You'd give it back, sometimes hurtling the junk at my face, but always giving back. I loved that you weren't afraid of me, like so many people are. You were smart, sharp, and just exactly what this company needed.

I admit, there were days when I wondered if I'd gotten under your skin and actually hurt you during our arguments. You have such a hard shell, I guess I'd convinced myself that you were fine and business was business. But I see now that I was wrong. And I'm sorry. Honestly, it really worries me that I made you believe we were enemies, that my childish actions caused you to doubt yourself and your worth (and don't say they didn't!) so much that you were confused when I proposed.

Well, honestly, I was confused too. I'd bought a ring on impulse about a week ago, and then on another whim, I found myself at your door tonight. Seriously, the words were out before I had a minute to realize what I was saying. And then you were angry, and it was just fail. From the moment I showed up at your door, it was all fail. You're right. I don't know you. I don't know anything about you, really. I mean, I thought I did. I thought being so close to you all year had shown me so much, but it didn't show me this side.

In my defense, I've never proposed before, and I doubt I will again for a long time. I feel like such a loser. Of course you'd deserve better than me. Of course you'd be wishing for a guy to come and sweep you off your feet, someone to say all those romantic things and give you flowers and all that. I'm shaking my head at my own narcissism in believing for ten seconds that you'd ever really fall for me, the awkward rich boy.

I know I'm rambling and not making much sense, but while I'm here, I have a confession to make. I guess I really don't know what love is. Sure, I understand family love—like with my sister and friends—but I'm completely lost when it comes to expressing myself, or even finding someone to express those feelings to. My mom and dad's relationship wasn't the best. She tried, but even her gentleness couldn't soften him. It didn't help that my dad was a workaholic who spent his whole life attempting to gain a vast fortune. Once he'd done that, he only wanted more and more and more… it was disheartening to watch. To lose him to greed and power like that. It still hurts me.

After my mom passed away when I was a teen, I decided to try to reach my father—have or build whatever relationship I could with him. So I did the unthinkable. After college, I joined his company. Soon, I moved up the ranks and developed my own. I allowed him to oversee and add his input when we broke off, hoping for a mutual respect and bond to grow, a like father, like son type of thing. It was him who recommended the consulting firm you work for, and how I came to hire you, though I didn't want to. I thought for sure my dad would become proud of me eventually, that this company would earn his respect, but it didn't. Instead, he only saw enough flaws to deem it necessary that I receive outside help.

I honestly shouldn't have treated you the way I did. And I certainly had no right falling for you, either. Forgive me, Eliza. I'm sorry to have you in the middle this crazy awkwardness.

Since writing the last part, I've taken a break and come back to the whole email. This is too long. I know it is. So I'll end it now. However, I have a small favor to ask of you. If you manage to read all of this, could you please consider remaining my confidant? My friend? My sounding board when things go rough, and—I don't know—I'm going to miss you. I've ruined everything, and I regret knowing that we'll never be the same again.

I'm sorry.
Forgive me.
Will

Eliza took some time as she stared blankly at the letter. For a few minutes after it'd been read, she sat in Will's arms and processed. Finally, she spoke. "You really are an introvert, aren't you?"

It seemed as though it was the last thing Will had expected her to say. "What?"

"You're shy. And not this debonair guy at all."

He snorted. "No. I've never pretended to be, either."

She bit her lip and nodded, her eyes blindly gazing at the white email before her. "You have no idea how to propose, do you? Have you ever had a real relationship before?"

"One where she wasn't attempting to scam me or take my money or make her parents happy? You mean, something where someone actually loved me for me?"

"Yes. That."

"No." He took a deep breath. "Until now. I hope?"

"That's another thing." She turned slightly to look at him. "Why in the world would you believe that if I read the rest of that email, I'd never speak to you again? What was that all about?"

He adorably shrugged and looked sheepish. "I don't know. I guess I thought if you knew more of the real me, you'd see the nerd that I am and wouldn't like me."

She rolled her eyes. "See? This is where we need to get our wires straightened out here. Vulnerability does not equal disgusting. Ever."

"Well, you were mad at me, too. Remember? I figured if you read it, you'd have more ammo or something. I don't know. I really don't know what I'm doing. At all. So can you help?"

Eliza's heart beat for the gorgeous man who gave so much to everyone else—and yet, didn't understand love. "You were crazy to be drawn to me. I could've hurt you so much."

"You did. But did it pay off?"

She leaned up and kissed his worries away. "Yes. So very much yes."

Will released a relieved sigh and collected her up. "Good. Because I don't know what I'd do without you."

After some time of butterflies and kisses, she asked, "So, are you going to finish what you were saying earlier?"

"Are you sure you're ready for this?" When she refused to answer, he grinned and cleared his throat. "I love you. And I can't imagine a life without you. I know that a week ago, I tried this and failed miserably. Well, that's because I was nervous and just assumed you'd want to marry me. Yes, I went about it all wrong. No, I'm not as conceited as I was then. However, my heart still beats for you." He got down off the bed and came around to her side. Then he bent on one knee and produced a ring out of somewhere. "Will you please set that heart to rest and marry me?"

He continued before she could respond, "I know you're worried if we'll be good to each other, and not become obsessed with money, and I really wanted a few more days or weeks or months to prove to you that we will be just fine. That in all this time since we've met, you didn't change—you only became better in my eyes. And hopefully, I've only become better in yours. And... I just can't wait any longer. If you'd like me to stop, I will but... until then, will you marry me?"

She looked down at that shy smile and those dark brown eyes and that perfectly flawed man below her, and she said the only thing a girl who was in love with him would say. "Yes. Of course I will." It was in that moment that she knew he was right. His heart was much bigger than any greed around him. With such an example of open arms, how could she ever fall?

"Thank you for seeing me, for choosing me. And especially for loving me. I really think I'm the lucky one here."

He sighed, as if he had been genuinely worried. But in the next second, he swooped her up and kissed her with the relief and security of a man who was most definitely and eagerly hers.

After some time, he pulled back, and her ragged breathing matched his. He murmured, "I'm afraid I have to warn you. Eventually, you'll meet my father."

"And?"

He shook his head. "At first, he's not going to be happy that I'm engaged to you. Chances are, he'll become like a tyrant maiden aunt—all honor and duty and rudeness. However, I'm pretty positive you'll win him over."

"And why's that?"

"Deep down, he loves feistiness."

She laughed. "Oh, I'm not worried about him. He can grump and moan all he wants, but I'm marrying you. Not him. So it really doesn't matter. Besides, your fate is worse than mine. Eventually, you'll have to meet Jane again—and I think that will be much more frightening."

He groaned and grinned and went to kissing her more. Which, of course, she didn't complain about, since that's exactly where she'd wish his lips to be anyway.

When Will finally pulled back he asked, "Now, the real question is, should we wake Melissa and Georgia and share our happy news? Or should we wait until morning?"

"Do you think they'd ever forgive us if we didn't?"

"Why do I have the feeling that our lives are always going to revolve around death threats from people who want us to act differently than we do?"

She chuckled, thinking of all her mom's threats. "Hasn't it always been that way? I know my life has."

"Yes, but you encourage it. I'm sure." He grinned.

"I definitely don't let it dictate what I'll do next."

"So you're saying not to tell them?"

Eliza glanced at one closed door and then turned toward the other. "Nah, let's surprise them tomorrow."

"Surprise us with what?" Melissa asked as she opened her door and yawned. "Out with it, you two. I'm not getting any younger."

Will winked at Eliza and then called over his shoulder, "We'll tell you in the morning, Mom. Now go back to sleep."

"Mom?" Melissa gasped. "Well, praise the Lord! I knew Vegas would do the trick! But do me a favor. Don't tell your father you've eloped just yet. We'll just plan a whole big wedding as if this never happened." She giggled. "It'll be our little secret."

THE END

Austen in Love #2

Jane and Bingley

CHAPTER ONE
On the First Day of Christmas

It was the Christmas wedding of the year—December 23rd. Simply everyone who was anyone was there. Jane glanced around the room for what seemed like the hundredth time that night. She swirled the rum-free eggnog in her pretty fluted wineglass and sighed. Her silver holiday dress—the one she spent a fortune on at Macy's—sparkled under the white fairy lights draped above her. There was laughter and joyous celebration all around. Everyone had come to her sister, Eliza's, wedding to Will Darcy. It was the most-anticipated and talked-about party this season, full of hope and happiness.

Except she wasn't hopeful, and she wasn't happy. Well—for herself. For Eliza, she couldn't be happier. No two people were more in love, or more ready for marriage than they were. And up until this moment—this exact past hour—it had been such a whirlwind of months and months of planning. Of contacting caterers and auditioning dresses, for that's really what trying on wedding dresses is—auditioning the very best one for the big day. Consulting hair, floral, photographers, caterers... the list went on and on. For what seemed like forever, this had been their biggest concern, and all that was talked about in the Bennet household.

Now it was over. Or almost over.

Jane rose her glass with the several others who applauded and sipped another toast to the couple. She wasn't paying much attention. Her toast was finished long ago, and with it was shed many tears of delight for her sister. But now... now there was nothing. Her last big part of the evening was over, and all that was left was a perfectly coiffed hairstyle, a glittering gown, and an empty seat next to her.

Her heart dropped as she finally glanced over to the calligraphy-written name card at her right. Charles Bingley. He hadn't come. After all his promises and those silly texts and emails assuring her they had much to talk about and to make up for lost time—all of that—it was over. He made it clear that not only did he not have time for his friend's wedding, but for the sister of the bride, either.

Jane's hand shook slightly, and she set the wineglass down. During the next applause, she stood up and carefully made her way through throngs of tables to the hallway of the elaborate rented building. If it wasn't for her dang heels, she would've taken the steps a bit quicker. She was almost to the restroom when she passed by a large darkened ballroom— one of its ornate French doors had been left open. It obviously had not been rented that evening. The empty room was too tempting to pass up. She needed a few minutes of peace and quiet to pull herself together, and what better place than an abandoned ballroom?

She slipped inside and allowed her eyes to adjust to the dark as she trailed the paneled wall with her fingertips. It was a little over a year ago that she and Charles had actually met. A year since she was immediately blown head over heels. He was perfect—they were perfect—or so she thought.

Everything came crashing down a few months later when he was assigned to open new offices in New York. It was then that Charles took her to lunch and told her it just wasn't going to work out. That being so far apart would put a strain on their relationship, and they needed to take a break.

That was eight months ago.

Eight long, ridiculous months.

She knew she was being impractical to even fall for someone she hardly knew, but then to still miss him eight months later was absurd! Honestly, what was wrong with her? She should've known that the first chance he had, he'd break her hope again. Yes, it was hope—not heart. She refused to acknowledge that her heart had been broken or would be broken by him again.

The stillness of the dark room seemed to envelop her as she walked farther into it. This was exactly what she craved— alone time. Being away from the bustling excitement. She had to process and take a few moments for herself before she came back.

So he had said months ago that they shouldn't date anymore. Lately, he'd been messaging, saying he'd missed her and was wrong and would like to start again. But with her hectic schedule—work and last-minute errands for the wedding, and his frantic New York schedule, they had yet to actually meet up. It was supposed to be tonight.

As in, a few hours ago. Which is why she'd splurged and purchased the silly dress and went all out on her makeup and hair and had butterflies in her stomach all day. Knowing he'd be watching her in front of everyone, during the ceremony, and really seeing her for the first time in months. It was nerve-racking and irrational all at the same time.

She couldn't find him in the massive crowd of people who had come, but she figured he would approach her. When he didn't, she rationalized the fact that Eliza had made sure he was sitting right next to her. If all else failed, she would definitely see him at dinner. But it failed. He wasn't there.

Her chest tightened, and she straightened her back before she let the panic of her stupidity overwhelm her. So what? So what if Charles didn't show up? What did it matter to her? Nothing. He was nothing. And he would continue to be nothing. She had no patience for players, anyway. Besides, there was probably a very good reason why he didn't make the wedding. Like, twenty of them, but why he did or didn't come shouldn't matter to her one bit. She took a deep breath and attempted not to overreact. The fact she was actually away from the crowd and hiding in an empty room proved she was being dramatic.

There was no drama here. None.

It was time to head back to the reception and smile and laugh and help where she could. Heaven knew, her mother was probably a nervous wreck, looking for her. Jane took a deep breath, turned toward the open door, and then froze. There he was. Standing in the room. His face was in shadow, but she would recognize his frame anywhere.

"Sorry. Forgive me. I didn't mean to startle you." Charles took a step toward her and then stopped. "I saw you leave and followed you in here."

"You—you did?" Her voice nearly cracked.

"Yes. You were so deep in thought, I didn't want to disturb you. Should I come back another time? We can definitely catch up later."

Jane's breathing was so erratic, she was positive he could see her heart pounding through her dress. He came. He actually came. And he'd followed her in here to talk to her. "When did you get to the wedding?"

"Just before the ceremony. I was running late and then got caught up with friends and family and was forced to sit with them during dinner. I know we were supposed to sit together, but . . . um… How are you? Are you okay?" He took another step forward.

For the first time, Jane Bennet actually had the urge to snap. He had been here the whole time? Since the ceremony over two hours ago, and he hadn't even come up and said hello? He was "caught" with family? And yet, he knew she was alone and waiting for him? Even if they were viable excuses, something about them seemed pretty lame.

If this was supposed to be their chance to start over, a whole lot needed to change. And it would have to be her who implemented it. She slowly walked toward him until they were nearly face-to-face in her heels. Then she slipped a hand under his tie and pulled him toward her. Gently, her lips met his for the first time in months. His faint cologne surrounded her.

She smiled as she felt him gasp and then released her hold. "Welcome back, Charles. I hope your flight went well." Their eyes met in the darkened room, and she let one eyebrow rise slightly. "I guess I'll see you around." Then she turned—before she lost her nerve—and walked out into the brightly lit hallway.

"Wait." He caught up with her as she headed back to the reception.

"Yes?"

It was as if he didn't know what to do. "Are you mad at me?"

"Nope." Her pace quickened as she smiled. "I'm happy to see you."

"And the kiss?"

She paused and glanced up at him. "Just a welcome home." She fiddled with the diamond watch at her wrist. "Look, I'm sorry. I've got to get back and help my family with everything. It was great seeing you."

Charles's jaw dropped. "Are you kidding? I thought we'd get to talk or something. You know, discuss *us*?"

Jane shrugged as she began to walk again. "Pity. So did I." She was clearly not his top priority—the fact that she had made him hers was enough. If he really wanted to put things right and get back together, he needed to step up his game.

She might still be the nicest girl he'd ever known, but she wasn't willing to be tossed aside again. He needed to realize her worth, or this relationship was over before it began. This time, Jane Bennet would be courted, acknowledged, seen, and cared about. She wanted a real man.

And she had every intention of getting him.

Coming Soon:

Austen in Love #3
My Persuasion

About the Author:

Jenni James is the busy mother of ten kids and has over twenty-five published book babies. She's an award-winning, best-selling author who works full-time from home and dreams about magical things and then writes about what she dreams. Some of her works include The Jane Austen Diaries (*Pride & Popularity, Emmalee, Persuaded...*), The Jenni James Faerie Tale Collection (*Cinderella, Snow White, Rumplestiltskin, Beauty and the Beast...*), the Andy & Annie series for children, *Revitalizing Jane: Drowning, My Paranormal Life, Not Cinderella's Type*, and the Austen in Love Series. When she isn't writing up a storm, she's chasing her kids around their new cottage and farm in Fountain Green, entertaining friends at home, or kissing her amazingly hunky hubby. Her life is full of laughter, crazy, and sunshine.

You can follow her on.

Facebook: authorjennijames

Twitter: Jenni_James

Instagram author Jenni James

Amazon Page (follow to get updates when a new book is released): http://www.amazon.com/Jenni-James/e/B003H0J9DE&tag=authorjennija-20

Subscribe to her newsletter: http://eepurl.com/FLYw1

She loves to hear from her readers. You can contact her via—

Email: thejennijames@gmail.com

Snail Mail:

Jenni James

PO Box 449

Fountain Green, UT 84632

Other books by Jenni James:

The Jane Austen Diaries

Pride & Popularity

Persuaded

Emmalee

Mansfield Ranch

Northanger Alibi

Sensible & Sensational

Regency Romance

The Bluestocking and the Dastardly, Intolerable
Scoundrel

Lord Romney's Exquisite Widow

Lord Atten Meets His Match (2017)

Cinderella and the Phantom Prince

Austen in Love

My Pride, His Prejudice

Jane & Bingley

My Persuasion

Modern Fairy Tales

Not Cinderella's Type

Sleeping Beauty: Back to Reality

Beauty IS the Beast

Children's Book:

Andy & Annie: A Ghost Story

Andy & Annie: Greeny Meany

Prince Tennyson

Women's Fiction

Revitalizing Jane: Drowning

Revitalizing Jane: Swimming (2017)

Revitalizing Jane: Crawling (2017)

Jenni James Faerie Tale Collection

Beauty and the Beast

Sleeping Beauty

Rumplestiltskin

Cinderella

Hansel and Gretel

Jack and the Beanstalk

Snow White

The Frog Prince

The Twelve Dancing Princesses

Rapunzel

The Little Mermaid

Peter Pan

Return to Neverland

Caption Hook

Other Books

Princess and the Pea

My Paranormal Life